Pink

Pink

ANCHOR BOOKS DOUBLEDAY

NEW YORK LONDON TORONTO SYDNEY AUCKLAND

Gus Van Sant

Pink

AN ANCHOR BOOK
Published by Doubleday
a division of Bantam Doubleday Dell Publishing Group, Inc.
1540 Broadway, New York, New York 10036

ANCHOR BOOKS, DOUBLEDAY, and the portrayal of an anchor
are trademarks of Doubleday, a division of
Bantam Doubleday Dell Publishing Group, Inc.

Book design by Claire Naylon Vaccaro
Illustrations by Gus Van Sant

Excerpts from *Great Skull Zero* by Lanny Quarles. © Lanny Quarles.
Used by permission.

The author gratefully acknowledges Jack Gibson for the use of the titles
and concepts *Cowboy Nemo, L.A. Cannonball, Teen, Brand New Cowboy,
TEX*ASS, Have You Seen My Ronnie Moore?, Thunder Mountain* and
Laughing District. © Jack Gibson.

The Library of Congress has cataloged the Nan A. Talese/Doubleday edition
as follows:

Van Sant, Gus.
Pink : a novel / Gus Van Sant. — 1st ed.
p.   cm.
I. Title.
PS3572.A42268P56   1997
813′.54—dc21   97-4110
                            CIP

ISBN 0-385-49353-3

Printed in the United States of America
First Anchor Books Edition: December 1998
10   9   8   7   6   5   4   3   2   1

To
the bosse of the
upper and lower tributarrys.
Goodbye. It's been good
to sea you. May you live
for river.

Pink

I think. I am a humble thinker. I am a man. I am a humble man. I am an industrial filmmaker. Once I was good, and now I am shamed. I have turned bad. I heed your call. I need help. I am looking for salvation. I am looking for the quick buck. I've sold out. I am spoiled by the system. I am not pure. Please save me. I spend the day trying to wade through the muck and mire of the local independent informmercial business where my clients all have bad breath, and wear gold chains around their neck, arms, wrists, (their privates?) and ankles. I have not met one client who does not have both gold and bad breath. Perhaps I have bad breath too. I must ask Jack, the kid that I met at the laundromat. Perhaps bad breath is why he doesn't pay that much attention to me and acts like he is trying to get away from me. I feel caught. I feel a midlife crisis sneaking up on me. I am scared. I am certainly alone. I feel odd, somehow, like a boat that's worked its way from the dock; ropes that were holding secure have become slack. I am drifting out to sea. I still trust I can find someone to help me. Miraculously, I still feel emotional attachments and there is reasonable discourse, I have not lost that ability, yet. I worry that I will . . . maybe soon. Wonder what that will be like, to not be able to relate to people any longer, or to talk in a normal fashion because your emotions won't act and react in appropriate ways for a sane disclosure. Most of all, I fear. I fear I will wake up soaked in my own fluids. I would fear books falling off the shelf onto my head but there are no more books on the shelf and I fear they will never be returned. I fear that I will be run over by a car driven by a man or woman who is running a red light at an intersection. I fear that Swifty's[1] bungee cord is going to snap and I will never see him again. I wish that I were an artist. I admire artists. When identity crises happen with them, they can make art out of it, sometimes it is better art than what they were making in the first place. But I fear artists. I fear art. I fear that the last bit of rusty wire holding the animals in their pens has snapped and the cows and goats are all slowly getting loose. Or that the gravitational pull of Saturn has lost its effect on me and I will go spinning off the surface of the earth toward the sun. I fear that perhaps most of all.

"Did you ever have to make up your mind?

"When the other thought's older and further behind.

"If you have the notion, to choose between time," I sang to myself, "did you ever have to finally decide?"[2]

The lyrics from a Lovin'

A drawing that accompanied the note

[1] Swifty is one of Spunky Davis' (the man telling the story) closest friends. They have worked together and know each other well. They have also been having a long-standing secretive affair.

[2] An inaccurate remembrance of John Sebastian lyrics. Spunky Davis, the man thinking these lyrics to himself, doesn't remember how the words go.

Spoonful song pass through my head as I look at a crumpled note in my hand. It is a message I found on the sidewalk on my way to the Tropicana Grill in downtown Las Vegas, and it reads:

Bruthas and Sistas of Las Vegas,

Make up ya minds. Are you going ta stay here wastin' time in Las Vegas or are ya comin' wit us inta the new dimension? Have faith. Make tha decision.
—The Two

There is a small drawing on one side of the note that looks like a skull. It is on a piece of ripped white paper, Xeroxed™ as if there are many of these messages. My interpretation is the note was perhaps part of a poster ripped from a nearby telephone pole that advertised a local rock and roll band. Or a Rave. Rave posters have exotic intergalactic or religious-communication themes. For what reason I do not know.

Folding up the note and stuffing it into my shirt pocket I pass through synchronized pneumatic doors and past two jocular bright-green-uniformed security guards on my way into the Tropicana Grill.

Listening to the musical sounds of nearby slot machines I find a seat and order breakfast. The walls are done up in a 1950s reflective stainless-steel tuck-and-roll diner theme, and it is so bright this morning that I have to put on my sunglasses as soon as I get comfortable on a red leatherette stool.

Thankfully this is my last day in Las Vegas. I have finished my week of shooting a series of Japanese knife

Spunky

informmercials and can't wait to be on my way back home to Sasquatch, Oregon.

Spending too much time in Vegas makes me nervous. Probably because of the horrible tragic accident that happened to my friend and favorite product spokesmodel Felix Arroyo[3] just a few months ago.

I pick up my fork, balancing a chunky portion of scrambled eggs on its four prongs, slip it into my mouth,

[3] By most accounts, Felix Arroyo, a young and talented product spokesman and informmercial presenter, had an aversion to a combination of mind- and mood-altering drugs, and died by misadventure in the gutter of the street in front of the nightclub

and bite down on one pesky little chunk of eggshell, and between bites feel the need to look at the little Xeroxed message I had put in my pocket.

I fish the note out and uncrumple it in my hand. I start to worry about the meaning. I suspect that it is a real message, meant for people of varying backgrounds, varying religions, straight or gay, didn't matter, or young or old, to come on a trip with a group of unknowns to a new place. The message asks the people to have faith about this other reality or other place.

Being in Las Vegas sort of ups the ante as far as possibilities of communications with space creatures are concerned.

I remember Sunday school, on another sunny day, when I was eight, my feet not yet able to touch the flesh-colored linoleum floor of the basement classroom where pictures of Jesus were hung on the wall. There it was posed that if we look at our dreams as alternate realities, and how infinitely fantastic they are, and if we can accept the dreams as part of reality, as real, then we can conceivably believe in any number of fantastic dimensions, as real. Other places similar to where we are now, but somehow more pleasant.

Other places. Like, say, Heaven. Or another world where secluded aboriginal tribesmen might live in Australia. Another world somewhere alive and prospering without our civilization's knowledge, perhaps on another planet.

Thundermountain, before an ambulance could be called to help him.

I'm not sure that this argument belonged in a Protestant Sunday school or was going to have a future in Protestant theology, but ever since that Sunday school class, I have believed in this larger fantastic, like, Reality, that we are all part of . . .

. . . brothers and sisters.

I put the note back in my pocket and realize that I never for sure know what is real anyway, because Reality is always moving off ahead of me and leaving me in a cloud of dust.

Overlooking the town of Sasquatch, the tower clock strikes eleven o'clock. It is a quiet town and we are still sleeping. Unless we are being bonged awake by the big tower bell.

"It is a *something* town," the Mayor—once a Mom and Pop grocery store clerk—says.

"Sasquatch is a city that works!" the County Commissioner proclaims, even though the city school board needs more financial assistance. The Governor of the State smiles on Sasquatch, the fairest of Oregon cities. The Governor keeps a house on the hill overlooking the city, and holds court on his balcony. For years this is a major source of gossip for the local papers, for if reporters place themselves just on the other side of the Governor's north retaining wall, they can hear the delicate discussions on the balcony.

But where am I?

Here I am, slumped over my desk. A fresh cup of instant coffee is steaming under my favorite picture of Felix Arroyo. It was Felix who had the idea to buy up the Amazon so lumber companies could not cut down the earth's last great forest. It was Felix who dreamed of getting all our friends together on a bus to produce our own informmercials, and damn Las Vegas dependence. Felix said a lot for someone in his early twenties. But he isn't talking much anymore, and it makes me sad.

"It's such a beautiful town," Christine Sigourney whispered over the phone as we talked about making a filmmercial for her new *Goldies* CD album before her bassist disappeared two months ago.

"Sasquatch really blooms in the spring, when the Chinese cherry blossoms all come out. I want flowers in the commercial . . . flowers . . . flowers . . ." She drifted off.

"It's such a beautiful town," she said. "It's such a sick town." Then she hung up.

It was flowers for the bassist and flowers for the filmmercial. Too bad. Christine's seen a lot of flowers lately.

"Are you awake yet?" I remember an early morning voice had said to me months and months ago.

"No," I said. It was a young man's voice.

"Then I'll call you back later." Just as he said that I realized the voice belonged to Felix.

Click.

If I had known that it was going to be the last time

I would ever hear his voice again, I would have woken up. Ashes. We all fall down. Someday.

"I'll call you back later," Felix said. Flowers. Flowers. He never called back.

Crossing a downtown Sasquatch street I run into the film school student named Jack.[4] Jack shows me the uncut reels of his new film which he calls *Don't Leave Me Georgetown*. The film is technically fucked up,[5] because of camera problems, Jack explains, but he is happy to have a camera at all, problems or no . . .

Jack and his friend Matt[6] and I screen *Georgetown* for ourselves in a screening room at the film school, which has made a cozy home for itself in a huge vacated Masonic Temple. The walls of the screening room are

---

[4] Jack is youthful, bright and cheery with thick glasses and a ponytail. He can't see very well without his glasses. Today he is wearing a red-and-yellow Chinese printed brocade jacket over numerous other layers of grungy clothing. This jacket is the big feature today in his wardrobe and it has pictures of little Chinese garden bridges, a little man with a black hat smoking a pipe (opium Spunky assumes is in the pipe), and there are a few stalks of bamboo and other plants growing around out of the pockets and across the lapel. Jack is in the company of his good friend named Matt.

[5] One might not have been too surprised at the technical mistakes since he is in school and is in the process of learning how to make

Jack

lined with gold-framed black-and-white pictures of omi-
nous-looking, pie-faced men who were the ruling "Drag-

---

films by trial and error. However, some of the mistakes are ex-
traordinary. There is a chattering of the image that is not related
to how Jack has threaded the projector. This chattering has the
images moving up and down so fast that one can only watch it for
brief periods of time before feeling sick. There is dust as well, and
so much of it that the viewer finds himself wondering how they
managed to put that much dust through the gate of the camera.
[6] Matt is curiously connected to Jack and it would appear to anyone, including Spunky, as if he and Jack have known each other
for a long time. They both wear interesting clothes that are worn
in complicated ritualistic layers. Matt has a beanie on, and his
topmost layer of clothing is a sweatshirt with a hood. He looks
more troubled than Jack, like he is capable of exploding at any
minute. Somewhat of a dark force. He is carrying an open beer in
a knapsack he wears around his shoulder so that he can get the

ons" of the temple. I think that the space they are using as the screening room may have originally been the Grand Dragon's office. Costumes and spears lie on the floor. There is also a single projector on a movable table that Jack has pointed at a wall painted white.

Jack and I discuss the many technical mistakes that we can identify as we watch the film. Almost everything is out of focus and the registration is unstable because of the way the film school cameraman loaded the film, so there are streaks of white like smeared halos coming off the tops of all the characters' heads.

"It works for me!" Jack says. He is beginning to like the registration mistakes.

"But, Jack, it is a mistake. You should find out what is wrong so you won't keep making the same mistake," I say, but when I look over at him he isn't listening. Jack's face is fixed in the permanent grin of someone who is being thoroughly entertained, mesmerized, by what he sees.[7]

He is a pretty good filmmaker, but he has to do some fancy editing.

Jack and Matt begin to tell me about a new script

---

bottle in and out of places where people may tell him that he cannot drink it, like the film school screening room. There is a definite possibility that there are more beers in the knapsack where the one he is drinking came from.

[7]But there is an absence of a smile, he has no smile, a characteristic that alerts Spunky to a strong similarity Jack has to Felix Arroyo.

they are writing when we are interrupted by a janitor who tells us that he is closing up the building.

"But I guess you can stay a little bit longer if you are in the middle of a discussion," the janitor says just before he catches Matt taking a sip from his beer and returning it to the knapsack. "On second thought, I think you all have to go now." Then the janitor tells Matt that he cannot drink beer in the film school.

Matt has a flat face. He has fierce, puffy eyes, eyes that are searching for something, anything, that might piss him off and send him into a youthful but angry Dadaist protest.

The story Jack and Matt begin to tell me is about superhero cowboys that go to a superhero convention. They refer to their original idea as Cowboy Nemo. We leave the film school and go to a Chinese takeout down the street. Matt pulls another beer magically out of his knapsack like a rabbit being pulled out of a hat.

We part after we finish eating from cardboard takeout containers. The strange thought of Jack's dusty out-of-focus film and the superhero convention idea makes me smile as I walk down the street.

The next day I try calling Jack from a number that he left with me on one of the Chinese takeout napkins. Next to the number Jack has drawn a cowboy hat. When I call the number no one answers the phone. I call repeatedly, and realize I will probably never see either Jack or Matt again.

Jack and Matt have moved. That is why I couldn't find them. Now I know where they are and how to get in touch; but they no longer have a phone. A filmmaker without a phone?

Matt (who I have decided is cute) has found a job pumping gas again, at Shell, which is one of the most irresponsible mega-company oil profiteers and tanker-leakers, according to Matt. I think that Shell owns the advertising agency that I do freelance work for.

Matt takes a sip of a beer and says slowly, "These mega-companies are banal, evil and slothlike, slowly absorbing everything in their path."

When Jack and Matt are together, Matt puts his arms around Jack, and kisses Jack's smooth ears and hands with tender little puffy-lipped kisses.

Matt

I hear more about their screenplay of Cowboy Nemo. All the characters in Jack's story have the same name, Nemo, but they have numbers to tell each other apart. They communicate one Nemo to another in a language called Envirese. Their superpowers are quite limited, I realize, and they are not cybertronic organisms as I'd once thought. They are humans with superpowers, but since the Nemos don't know how to use their powers, they have a superpower convention, where they are able to learn how to manage their superpowers. It is a place to teach the Nemos some incredible things about themselves, like how to fly or levitate or use their mind recording[8] and whatnot.

The Nemos have traveled from different states, countries and worlds to meet each other in Nemo Land. After an amusing competition which includes levitating a fifteen-foot-high steel ball in the air, the winning Nemo has to stay in Nemo Land after the convention breaks up. The only Nemos left in Nemo Land at the end of the story are the winners from the past years, although the winner in 1989 left (escaped) by getting a janitor to let him out a secret trapdoor. The 1989 winner has returned to his old hometown and become an alcoholic. Why, I don't know. Jack hasn't told me that part yet. I don't know if Jack has worked that part out yet.

"They cannot fly," Jack told me. "They can't. But they can levitate off the ground for brief periods of time, like, if they try levitatin' really hard. Like, say, they can hover seven inches off the ground 'bout ten seconds, but only with an unbelievable amount of effort. This levitatin' has a side effect though. When a Nemo levitates, an intense buffetin' noise envelops them and the area they are in."

---

[8] Inside of every Nemo is the ability to record any piece of visual or aural info for storage and eventual playback. Although there is a limited amount of storage space, the Nemos find mind recording useful especially when traveling great distances where they need a lot of directions.

Curious. Maybe Jack is stoned. He sounds like he's completely stoned, doesn't he?

It is possible that they are stringing me along with this Nemo story. Sometimes it's hard to tell if they aren't just pulling my leg about it. It wouldn't surprise me if they actually double over in hysterics after I leave and am safely out of sight. This doesn't make me any less interested in the story of Cowboy Nemo, however. It even makes it more interesting if they are making all this stuff up off the top of their heads.

That's one sequence of Cowboy Nemo. They should write the screenplay.

Later in the week I run into Jack downtown in front of a fountain in Paranoid Park. I tell Jack that I will pay him to write a screenplay about the Nemos, but he's not interested. Something about the sound of money that doesn't sit right with him.

(Perhaps a trade?)

He says that I don't have to pay him and leaves it at

that. I am going to ask him again. But I have to locate him and as I mentioned, he has no phone.

Driving to my office I see Jack riding on the back of a motorcycle.

I yell from my car window, "The

money is so you don't have to
get a job," I say, and he disap-
pears down the street talking
to his friend driving the motorcycle.

Maybe he will think this
over. The idea of having to
take a job must be so dreary
to him that I think he will reconsider the offer. Or perhaps he is considering just
how much money he could
get away with. Money that I don't have. He might be
holding out until I offer more.

I haven't offered any amount yet, just hinted. He is a hippie and I'm sure doesn't think too hard about money.

He could write with Matt.

I catch up to the motorcycle in traffic and yell out my car window again to Jack.

"You can write with Matt," I say. "Then Matt wouldn't have to pump gas!"

A warm body to keep him company. They could write together.

I discuss this with him, and it is beginning to sound vaguely acceptable to Jack. But his overall reaction, or underlying "vibe," is one of suspicion.

I try to talk in their language and say enthusiastic things like, "It's gonna be far out." They look at me with more suspicion. If I were them I too would be suspicious of an overweight balding man wearing a tan overcoat and shiny brown loafers, who is all of fifty-two, and carries an umbrella. Men like me are always suspicious when talking to younger men, or the type of older boy that Jack and Matt appear to be.

♠

What exactly went on with those two rock and roll stars, Blackie of the band Dill and Blake[9] of Speechless? Looking into the many facts Florida teenagers feel compelled to, we find the reported lost husband Blake wasn't really lost at all, as was alleged. Blackie actually knew where he was. He was back in Stubtown, after having escaped from his rehabilitation center in Orlando. Blackie knew her husband/star was on the lam from an inside scoop by some reliable sources, one of whom was

[9] Felix's and Blake's earnings had been enough that if you combined them you would have enough money to buy the town of Sasquatch. Their deaths happened near enough together that one had a feeling they were somehow connected. Both suffered enormous strain from all the machinery that was built up around them (in Blake's case, literally), sometimes from their own doing. They mattered so much to so many people that they felt older than their years. And with so much strain, both of them needed to let off steam, and party every now and then. But the partying overtook the responsibilities of being who they were and they died from partying. In a way. At least that was Felix's case. Blake seemed to have a strange idea of partying, his idea of a great party was to hole himself up in some remote glove compartment where nobody could find him, and just sit there ordering things over the phone that would send him into bankruptcy. That was his idea of partying.

Blake's roommate in his rehab center and who knew exactly where Blake went and was telling whoever would listen. This guy, or squealer, was an infamous rehab fixture who went by the name of Lonnie Trax and whoever found themselves in rehab might have run into this character. He was the lead singer and front man for the band Nude Chester, which had been touring as an opening act for the late said band Speechless.

Some members of Speechless had had it with Blackie and Blake problems. They continued to recognize that he was their front man and leader but the other countless band members[10] wouldn't put up with Blake's selfish shenanigans any longer, and were thinking of breaking up the band.

A private eye that Blackie had put on the case started thinking that he was hired by Blackie as a red herring, and that there were altogether other things on her mind beyond simply finding where her husband had disappeared. Which sounded possible to the public. The public, following this story closely, would at this time have believed anything at all about Blackie, like, man, they could have read that she was really Neil Armstrong in drag, and they would have believed it with a shrug. The chips were beginning to stack up against Blackie. She was the chick who had done our rock star wrong. She was the Yoko Ono of the early-to-

[10] Some figured there were eighteen in all but nobody was sure.

mid-nineties rock scene, and everything was apparently her fault.

Blake was trying to push the monolithic rock and roll millstone just enough to get his album higher on the charts, and proceeded to indulge in reading and rereading every piece of criticism ever written about him or his band. He was attempting to decipher what he privately called the asskiss factor, which was a term Blake used for a sort of popularity curve, which up until this time refused deciphering, though every rock act is trying to crack the code all the time. He had been successful enough that he thought if anyone could break the code and prevent an album's decline from the top of the *Rolling Stone* charts, he might be able to do it. This was, in effect, to save his relationship with his approximately eighteen-member band and with his wife. Although he was unable to look any of them in the eye and tell them that he cared, he

The Caterpillar 953 WDA Track Loader without sun bonnet

really did secretly care only about them, and about his own popularity, of course, which included them.

In the original Punk manifesto written at CBGB's sometime in the mid-seventies Popularity still came first. And with Blake his band and his wife and his triplets[11] were definitely second in line, after himself. That was what bugged him the most.

Blake walked along the middle finger of an eight-lane east-and-west-bound thoroughfare on a warm Orlando afternoon. He was following the sun, which was setting somewhere on the other side of the municipal airport, which he could tell was nearing because of the earsplitting approach pattern of behemoth jets practically knocking Blake on the head with their rubber tires. His legs lifted one after another out of overgrown median grass as if helium balloons were attached at his ankles and lifting his tired rehab feet forward one after another plop-plop-plop, involuntarily.

He was dazed after running in an evasive pattern of his own design which he needlessly but methodically put to work to ensure his escape from the minimum-security Cloudy-Bright Rehabilitation Center there in Orlando. Somebody had helped him over the eight-foot wall, could have

---

[11] Blackie had given birth to three identical boys two years prior to Blake's last U.S. tour. The boys were named Bill, Binky and Bartholomew.

been Lonnie. Which meant Mr. Trax could be tossed out for that, Blake was thinking.

As Blake pranced down the median with cars hissing by on both sides, he came to an awful and depressing realization. These people who were driving by him in their cars, who were probably listening to his songs on the radio, and who would just as soon run over him as though he were a stray dog (he was a stray dog) needed him. These people needed him. They needed his identity. He could hear the roar of the crowd. The crowd seemed to be coming from the car radios and could be heard above the four screaming turbine engines overhead wowing in their Doppler loss and gain. These crowds needed him. They needed his life, they needed his shit.

Because they had no lives of their own. Sad but true.

They had no identity of their own. They needed Blake to tell them what to believe in. They needed someone to follow. Like sheep. And he was their shepherd, which also pissed Blake off.

"Fucking sheep," he mumbled as he walked and loped.

They were his followers, Blake thought as he stumbled over a paper Super-Gulp tossed in his way as he crossed the road.

"They need me. They need me more and more. I can't help them," Blake said aloud but the people inside their cars couldn't hear, so that he looked pathetic and hopeless, drooling about these sheep/fans and tripping across the Super-Gulp on his way to the storm fencing by the side of the road, his face beet red from the setting sun and his own annoying whimpering.

But the realization came to him as it had been coming recently, "I cannot save myself."

To what extent his life's eventual downward spiral was precipitated by its true outcome and destiny, in retrospect, no one could say.

There seemed to be a number of contributing factors to this dire situation:

1. His wife was leaving him.
2. His wife had not left him yet.
3. His album was descending, ebbing, losing it.
4. Heavy machinery.
5. Blake thought a rival rock star, Tony from

Cream Spinach, was screwing his wife and . . .

6. Tony's album was on the top of the charts.

It seemed inevitable that the balloons tied metaphorically to his feet would be carrying him up and over the clouds soon now. And that would be that.

During his rock and roll shows he used to be able to make his guitar say things like, . . . Hello! Boise, Idaho! . . . he could stretch the notes so they formed humanlike sounds and make his guitar speak! There was one time on the tour that he made his guitar say, Fuck you, I hate y'all and I want to die. That specific message however was directed at the sound man and the rented PA system but the rock writers didn't care, they found other meanings to it. So many creative and classic rock and roll stadium gestures have been born out of horribly malfunctioning rental PA systems.

He couldn't write words but he could make his guitar talk. He didn't need to write words because he could scream shit, and that scream could make the hairs on the back of your neck stand up and try a run for it out the flat gray stadium exit doors.

Blake walked on, he stepped, with balloon steps, over a curb that separated the median from asphalt and continued onward in a peculiar stumble, or prance, bouncing off the chain-link fencing and toward the airport.

Delta Air Lines flight number 189 was leaving out of Orlando to Nashville then on to Stubtown. Blake had been repeating the plane's departure time at seven-thirty in the evening, gate sixteen, over and over again in his head so he wouldn't forget.

His blond hair jostled out of the way as he looked up at signs that guided the traffic to the right, into a circle of confusion which was Friday airport traffic. He was beautiful. He had the most beautiful eyes. And he had the most beautiful confused look on his face.

Pink

❖

I am inviting Matt and Jack to join all my friends at a gay barbecue in the coming weekend at a rock promoter's house. They can put on their lovey-dovey act for all the queens. That might get ugly, though. Oh well, everything gets ugly eventually.

Ben[12] says, "Maybe Jack and Matt's lovey-doveyness isn't an act." But I cannot seriously believe that they are in love. They love, but are not in love. That's it, I think.

Kids today, who can tell. Maybe they are in love. Matt and Jack. Maybe love is part of it. Part of the big picture. The big picture is getting bigger all the time. I don't like to think about the big picture.

On another day during a discussion about writing Cowboy Nemo, Jack never moved from an intense stare

[12] Ben is a guy who designs the sets for Spunky's informmercials. Ben is thin, Spunky is fat. Spunky is slow and Ben is fast, Ben's clever, Spunky, ponderous. They make an interesting pair as they walk down the street. When they are working, Ben always is talking about boys, he never stops talking about boys. He also sometimes refers to an imaginary creature called the Boy. The Boy is a mysterious reference to a generic totem to all boys in all lands that Ben worships on the altar of the Boy. Ben is somewhat kinky. But he is not considered overly so. There are times when Spunky loses touch with Ben. There are times when Spunky thinks that Ben is avoiding him. And Spunky is inclined to slink back, and to not press the issue of being in the company of Ben.

at the river. He only responded to overtures of work with quiet little "yeah"s and "uh-huh"s as if I were bothering him. As if I were asking him to make love to me. As if I wanted to fuck him. (Or fuck him over.) I found out the reason for his forlornness was that a close cultural icon of Jack's named Blake had committed suicide the day before. He is apparently well known in the younger musical culture.

Jack's face reflected the water as if it were made of chrome or glass. I started to think he looked like Felix Arroyo. I thought that my initial attraction to Jack in the first place was that he looked like Felix.

Jack sometimes wears a black T-shirt with little rips in the front made by hand and of his own doing. Rips made by a razor. Little razor rips. The picture emits a kind of tattered quality. Jack's hair is thick and greasy enough that he can style it just about any way he wants, he can make it go straight up in the air like a fright wig. But for now his hair is pulled back into a bun! He is what you would call sensitive. Then Jack's skin, the most revealing thing, he has skin that is permanently tanned, and possesses rather large pores. A feature that is identical to Felix. He is Felix. He is Felix's double. Unbelievable! If only our friends could see.

Speaking in a very low, soft voice, Jack blurted, "Styrofoam cup manufacturers, like, run a dull but, like, intensely profitable business, like evil, which is intensely dull."

Blurting! Another alarming similarity!

He, Jack, also possesses a face that reminds a person of a Japanese cartoon: Felix—same cartoon thing, a heart-shaped jawline, tussle of hair hanging down over their foreheads, a sleepy puffiness around the blue eyes and winning (smileless?) smiles.

And Jack loves. He is love. He is walking love. He seems to care and look compassionately at everything around him, which is another physical duplication.

These doubled things fascinate me. The double ears. The double hands, the double voice, but it is not him. It is not Felix, and it is awkward to think this. It might be unfair to Jack.

I think that Jack is aware of the confusing likeness. I think that he wants to talk to me about it, but is afraid.[13]

Another eerie characteristic is that Jack has a group of friends besides Matt who are with him a lot, like traveling minstrels, they are banded together as a cohesive and cozy nest of like-minded comrades.

Oh, Jack said that besides his friend Blake's death sending him into a funk, he was banned from renting the film school's camera. He was in trouble, or was having trouble, I couldn't hear all of what he said exactly. This equipment rental blacklisting was a penalty for an up-

---

[13] In fact Jack is aware of his likeness to Felix. It is actually a large part of his life. Because of the informmercials, Jack has said "I'm not him" to people who ask. Felix was well known in Jack's community in Texas. And other people besides Spunky have noticed the way that Jack looks almost exactly like Felix Arroyo.

setting display at an awards ceremony. Jack said that strange rumors had been circulating around the film school that he had walked onto the stage to accept an Umpire Award with no clothes on.

I would have paid to see that.

And he said that the "Sponsors" were insulted. I couldn't figure out who the Sponsors were. Probably Liberty Films, that would be ironic.

What angered the Sponsors, I think, was, after Jack had gone up on the stage to accept his award, Matt had followed him up there and pulled his pants down. He mooned the Sponsors, that is, after he kissed Jack for a minute onstage and put the entire microphone in his mouth and moved his head back and forth as if he were giving it a blow job.[14]

If the Sponsors were upset, he got the right people angry. No one else seems to have minded, though, ex-

---

[14] The reason that Matt did this was because he thought that the Umpire Award attendees were taking themselves too seriously, and was disgusted with the lavishness of the show which included synchronized dancing Lennon Sister look-alikes and a jazz band dressed up as if they were an Army unit taking a cigarette break. Matt thought the ceremony, which included a small nod to the film school by offering an award to them, was too much about money and profit, since most of the awards were presented for commercials and industrial films. Which Matt misunderstood. The reason that the Umpire Awards ceremony honors commercials and industrial films is because those are the only types of films that are made in the town of Sasquatch, Oregon.

cept the film school was embarrassed that the Sponsors were angry so now they won't let Jack rent any more equipment as recompense for the upset.

"Think of the price of film!" Jack said. I don't know why that blurted out.[15] He blurts occasionally.

Stoned maybe.

He said that someone was going to write an article about the whole thing, and I asked, "Who?" And he laughed (rare).

He said, "I don't know, man."

He didn't know . . . it was just a rumor, and I'm asking him like a hmm/professional who knows the press article is one thing, but *who* writes the article is another.

He doesn't know this. A boy like Jack, who is a twenty-one-year-old Austin hippie who looks just like my dead friend and compadre, Felix Arroyo,[16] wouldn't automatically know these details about publicity. Jack might have to learn more about publicity if he and Matt continue behaving like this.

These are reasonably marginal kids. They will use

---

[15] He was making a reference to the photographers who were taking pictures of the award winners. Matt's display was something worth taking a picture of but Jack thought the photographers were holding back because they didn't want to use too much film. One could see his point. But this was another misinterpretation, because the photographers were not trying to save film, they were just in shock and didn't respond to Matt's antics fast enough.

[16] Felix Arroyo was lost to the world in a horrible accident, one that none of his closest friends could see coming, as accidents

words like "man" or "dude" in every sentence without thinking. Would you think that pulling down your pants at an awards ceremony is a sign of unruliness? Maybe I am not as up to date, but you could think that it was a sign of something . . . I find it engaging . . . one part of me definitely thinks it is a sign of extreme forthrightness and intelligence.

Jack looked across the water as a purple sunset beat the city of Sasquatch back into darkness.

Pink

---

can happen sometimes, and one in which it was impossible to re-cover from, or reverse, as all of those who knew Felix were painfully aware of. They wanted to somehow turn the clock back so that the news and actuality of Felix's death hadn't happened, and wasn't being written about in the *Las Vegas Daily News*. This eventuality, Felix's death, is one thing that Jack is intending to rectify later.

Πινκ αλτ. υνιϖερσ.

I am lying in a bed inside a mansion in a big city. There is a plastic pillow on the bed. And I am thinking and feeling how very fragile life is. All life. Even life that you thought was the strongest thing in the world, suddenly it seems very fragile. With people shooting things, flying around in planes and bungee jumping all over the place. I want to learn about how fragile all the world is. I want to learn about it, so I can try to help it.

Dear Brutha,

There is this infomercial fella, Spunky, who talks like he is gonna take a shit at any second. He is kinda weird, I mean, you gotta take him in short visits but I think he is sending out signals, like we might want to get to know him a little betta, I don't know why, but I think he is sending the signals. Matt wants to get to know him, said that he thinks he knew him on the otha side, me too. I think that I mighta known him too. I wish you'd tell us more about the old level, I can't rememba a thing.

Some of this business is hard to get used to after our previous levels of travel. I feel kinda sad, kinda let down because I heard from Matt that he used to be one of my favorite rock and roll playahs before I was on tha new level.[17]

---

[17] The level that Jack is writing about is the stacking level of a dimension they call Pink which he and Matt are learning to control

It is good that he is here with me now, we can take care of eachotha, Brutha, but we gotta get to know eachotha betta. Maybe we can jam togetha. It's funny bein' on tha road with this cat, but he is fuckin' crazy, drinks his brains out, and neither of us know much about what went on before we were travelas for your racket.

Speakin of da racket. We are just starting to go out and recruit potentials for entry into level 2 courses. You had given me this idea which I'm gonna do, where we will have meetin's with folks in small sessions, like neighborhood-style sessions, and we'll give little speeches about where we want to take them. Tell them the truth, doncha think? Well, I already did one, doncha know, where this small group of people in my neighborhood had a potluck, dat's where all the people in the neighborhood bring their own pot to the party, ha-ha, only kiddin'. No, they had this little party and we gave them the lowdown, and they ate it up. Half of them said they had been waitin' for something like this to happen. Just like one-two-three, they all signed up and gave us their shit, like their money and shit. We will keep workin' it and keep you posted. Meanwhile we have to make these films for film class . . .

---

as part of their beginners' education in handling movement and manipulation of time and space travel. They aren't that good at it yet, but it's pretty hard. To differentiate between linear time, Pink terminology uses the word "stacking." Stacking levels is a way for interval time to be differentiated from connection-oriented linear time, which is to say that there is no time in the dimension of Pink.

Hey, this film student gig is real good, we are completely taken for real, fuckin' A. But you shoulda showed us how to spell, not that it's even so bad, we almost fit right in wit da bonehead students here. I been tellin' the gay infomercial director all about the imaginary stories that I wanna make. Hope he doesn't put the moves on me. I can handle myself, though.

Hey, Brutha, maybe we can do some movie shootin' when we get home, I'd like that, make a movie, been thinkin' up this concept called Nemo, I'll communicate witcha layta.

Okay, that's all for now, I hope they don't pick up on these transmissions, but I guess you got all that worked out, huh, you pretty smart fella, okay, bye.

peace, Jack

The light outside is subdued. It is good light, what little of it there is. Some people here in the town of Sasquatch need to keep lights on in the day so they don't become deprived of light, and slip into a dangerous soul-searching funk that often ends in shooting oneself or jumping off a bridge. We need light up here, and lots of it. Maybe that is why we are so good with stage lights and television lighting.

Television stage lighting and an expertise in the science and artistry of stage lighting are perhaps why Sasquatch is the originator of the informmercial. Before Las Vegas got into the business of making informmercials. We are some of the only people who stay inside, out of the rain, long enough to make them. We are some of the only people who stay inside long enough to watch them.

Oh! Flash and a half, Jack just called! Oh-my-God . . . he said that he can come with Matt to the barbecue, Spike[18] had to ride over to their house on his bike to tell

---

[18] Spike. He is a very cheery amateur informmercial presenter. He is going for the big time, but he is still making his way mostly by jerking espresso in the downtown espresso store. He is short for his age, and was having an identity crisis about his height. Spike recently had new pictures taken for his new head shot, so he could get more informmercial jobs. He was looking forward to going on some casting calls but worried that they may still think that he is

them to call me because they don't have a phone. This is an easy thing to get Spike to do, because I think that they have pot laying around, and Spike can pinch a bud off one of them. He loves doing that.

Only one thing is wrong, Matt might be pumping gas tomorrow. Bummer (I am beginning to talk just like they do). Oh well, it would probably turn into a bad scene anyway. They would no doubt embarrass me in front of my friends. Using words like "man," and smoking pot and kissing each other but not meaning it the way that my friends mean it. But something inside me likes to be embarrassed.

I am addicted to being embarrassed, that's it! Perhaps in the same way they are addicted to their pot. I just realized it.

Does everyone feel this way?

I've run out of things to write about Jack, I have to gather more information.

I run into Matt downtown in front of Kelly's Bar.

Matt might have a drinking problem. If he weren't so young I would say that he definitely has a drinking prob-

---

fifteen. He gritted his teeth when he said, "I am not fifteen," as if fifteen were some sort of curse on him. He is unaware that for some people it would be a blessing if they could say that. But he has always looked fifteen and even now, at twenty-six, he looks like a cute blond-haired fifteen-year-old. Sorry, Spike.

lem. Matt was a professional skier in his younger days, when he was a teen. I wonder if Matt was beaten by his father when he was younger. Someone must have beaten him, he is so hyperactive. If they didn't, then he is beating himself, for his father.

Matt says his father is writing a book.

"It is to be a roundabout discussion, like, of the color pink. It is a book that my father is always writing and is never finishing," Matt says.

"My father, who is a pretty laid-back cat, says it is about the color of the Beverly Hills Hotel, where he spends a lot of his time when he's not in Austin, Texas. "It's also," he says, "the color in utero."[19]

Does he know about that? Is he about to tell me that he has a girlfriend? I hate it when they tell me that.

"Pink is a color that marks the highest degree of awesomeness or perfection," Matt says. "As when you say you are 'in the pink.' It is, as well, the color of movies when the color fades."

I knew that.

"I know that . . ."

"It was also Judy Garland's favorite color, did ya know that? It is the color of the painted walls in a drunk tank, a color that calms them at first but eight hours later

---

[19] Matt is only having a little fun with Spunky, because he is assuming that this reference to women's private parts will make Spunky uneasy, and he is right about that, plus he is taking pleasure in making up a relatively complicated fib, just for the sport of it.

it begins to drive them insane if they are not already insane to begin with." Matt smiles insanely.

I assume Matt knows quite a lot about the drunk tank.

"I guess you know a lot about that, huh?" I say, and he continues to smile dementedly.

"It was the color of the Roman Empire. It is the gay color . . ." Dum-da-da! Right on, Matt.

". . . it is the color of power, and, like, the color of sex and it is also the color of pigs; which my dad has a special affinity for. Pigs, man. He loves pigs," Matt says.

From what Matt is telling me, I think his father is a pig farmer. He is an eccentric who loves pigs.

"It was in the Beverly Hills Hotel over dinner that I first heard about his book, and my dad was telling me that I should consider making a film out of this book, *Pink*. He talked for an hour about the color pink, but, man, a lot of what he said I couldn't hear because he didn't talk loud enough." Matt shook his head as if this were a terrible tragedy. He really is acting strangely. So mysterious. I am not sure that all of it is true or if some of it is being made up for my benefit. Matt . . . So much stuff seems to be made up off of the top of people's heads and then presented as if it has been around forever.

When I ask Matt about the book and if I can read it, he says, "My father has been talking about *Pink* for a long time, but there is no actual book; he only talks about it." What the hell?

"It is about three awesome buildings," Matt continues, "the Beverly Hills Hotel, the Royal Hawaiian Hotel and his mother's house. These buildings are all pink. A few months later, inside of his ranch house in Texas, I came across a book filled with blank pages, bound in, like, pigskin, to be filled with his story about buildings. Embossed in gold shit was its title, *Pink.*"

Back to Jack, brothers and sisters. Lately Jack is writing a new script, it is called TEEN. And it is about a teen idol. Did he just make this up? He says that Matt is going to be the lead in TEEN. I say that Matt is twenty-two, not a teen. How is he going to play a teen? Jack seems to think his age, twenty-two, is okay. Jack? . . . He says that Matt looks like Brad Pitt. I think that Matt looks like Harpo Marx. We disagree on these points. But Matt is twenty-two, no doubting that. Isn't that a problem if he is going to play a teen?

Jack says, "Look at Luke-goddamned-Perry, he's like forty and he's playing a high school kid!"

I didn't know that. Which is Jack's point. I reconsider. Of course he is right.

I ask him whether, in the script, the teen idol takes drugs and dies (I was thinking of Felix and I think Jack was forced to, too). Jack says, "No, he just gets knocked down by a fan."

Ha-ha-ha . . . he gets knocked down, that cracked me up. It's been days since I've had anything to laugh about. Or perhaps weeks. I don't remember when I laughed last. Jack looks at me as if this pathetic little tidbit of humor doesn't deserve a laugh. He doesn't know what to make of such an easy audience and is worried by my limited taste. I want to see the script but he says it isn't finished yet. Hmm. My suspicion increases.

Jack says, blurts, I think for my benefit, that he has a low opinion of books, that they are just piles of stones set up to show coming travelers where other minds have been, or at best signal smokes to call attention.[20]

. . . stoned . . .

"So what else?" a distant, soft Felix voice would murmur, through a shaky connection that spat and buzzed. "What else?" he would say over the phone, a few days before he met his unscheduled Thundermountain fate.

"Uh, I don't know . . ." I would say, twisting the stringy yarn on the end of an Afghan rug that wove representations of Russian tanks and machine guns into its pattern.

"Tell me something," he would say.

"Well, I took a drive today and I ran into my old boyfriend."

"Yeah?"

"And I didn't know what to say."

"Maybe you shouldn't say anything," Felix would suggest.

---

[20] Jack was stealing this quote from John Muir, founder of the Sierra Club, who wrote that he had a low opinion of books. However, he wrote seven of them. Hmm.

"There was a heavy vibe, I wanted to just talk like we used to talk, but no way."

Then Felix'd say, "That's fascinating," like maybe it really wasn't.

"No, I never know what the fuck to say to them when they know so much about you . . ." I would say.

Idle chatter, which didn't mean anything but it was the sound that two warm bodies made at the end of the scratchy remote-phone line.

Felix was an old friend although I hadn't known him for very long. He had an interesting face. A darkish complexion, with large pores and naturally dirty blond hair that was beginning to turn brown. His hair went up in a large Doo-Wop number high on his head, which was a sort of trademark look for him in all of his on-screen work. Felix loved to tell stories. His idea of fun was to sit around for twenty-four hours and have a marathon storytelling session. His friends were all storytellers, and Felix himself was one of the best.

My favorite Felix story was the one about a bumpy transatlantic flight where he sat nervously across the aisle from an overwrought hysterical lady who was flying for the first time in her eighty-year life.

"The lady wore a black silk blouse and a choker of real pearls, and she was whimpering and shivering and looking nervously about the cabin, her fear of death plainly fixed on her wrinkled face in a fiendish fright mask," Felix explained.

"Then suddenly she'd see something out the window that would alarm her as she flew at six hundred miles an hour five thousand feet above the ground." Felix jumped up from his chair, as if he was still fixed by an imaginary seat belt.

"'Oh heavens!!!' she would scream. 'Looookk!!!' pointing distractedly out the window of the plane, her fright mask moving and stretching across her hysterical face." Felix would pantomime. "'My God!!! Loooookkk!!! It's a plane!!!!' she would bellow, 'A PLANE . . . IT'S A PLANE!!!!'

"And me, I start to get freaked out," Felix says with a certain gesture pointing all his fingers at his head as if lightning bolts are coming from it, "on the edge of hysterics myself, and unable to control my curiosity, I immediately get wrapped up in her intense, phobic, clinically certifiable hallucinations. Looking at where the woman was pointing, I could see what she saw. It was a plane flying the other direction.

"In her hysterics, however, she was not seeing a plane flying the other direction, she thought she was looking at a plane that was having engine troubles. An airliner that was going down in flames, or going down because its engines had wearily given out from simply flying too long and far. Or," Felix would explain, "in her imagination the plane could be falling from the sky because its wings had been ripped off by some strange wind or cloud monster.

"'It's . . . it's . . . it's . . .' she stuttered and gaped again at the little plane flying the other direction, '. . . it's . . . DESCENDING!!!'" Felix said.

"Her genteel British husband, who wore a neatly pressed pinstriped banker's-blue suit, and sported a thick sweeping brushy-white mustache, would put his arm around his whimpering lady wife and console her.

" 'No, no, dear . . . no, it's just flying along, dear. See?' he would say to her, with his hand mimicking a kind of happy going-about-its-own-way gesture, tracing it through the air in front of the window. 'See, dear, it's just flying along normally.'

"The woman would calm herself to a quiet bumble-bee buzz, but as she watched the plane out the window the fear would build up and she would explode again. Making almost no sense.

" 'No it's not!!!' she said, tearing off her seat belt and rising out of her seat. 'It's descending!! IT'S DE-SCENDING!!!' She would be screaming, crying and whimpering all at once, her face splintering into as many different expressions of fear as there were reasons not to be flying in the first place. In the grip of her horror she would insist, 'It's descending!!!!!!!'

"A flying paranoiac myself, I would then tune into her fear-dream and start communicating through para-noiac antennae a stuttery language common only to me and the woman. 'Where!!!' I would shout," Felix shouted.

" 'There!! There!! You can see we . . . we're descend-ing!!!' She would yell as she involuntarily shook.

"Of course, the plane that she was looking at was an-other plane. But through her shattered logic she was watching her own plane, which she was convinced without a doubt was descending right in front of her eyes. She could have seen anything out the window and she would have thought that it was a picture of herself, or the vehicle that she was in. If she saw a"—Felix would search for the right illogical object for his example of how insane the woman had become—"seal! If she saw a seal out the window, she would have thought that she was flying in a seal!

"Her husband would look across the aisle at me with an angry expression that communicated silent fiery words, like, 'You are only making her worse, please stop listening to her.'

"And the gentleman would coax the woman back into a seated position, but she remained audible, making a kind of running-water sound, like, 'ooooohhhhhh . . . oooooooo uuuuuhhhh . . .' and trembling.

"Then," Felix would tell a hotel room full of story listeners rapt with attention, "later, in the middle of the night during the cross-continental ten-hour flight, I was fast asleep, and suddenly the plane hit some seat-shaking turbulence that woke me out of a deep sleep, brothers and sisters.

"I had put my eye blinders on when I went to sleep, so when I woke up, I thought I was dead and being shaken around in a black turbulent vortex. I stood up in the plane ripping the eye blinders from my face and wailing, 'HOLY MOTHERFUCKER!!!' "

When Felix lifted the blinders from his eyes, he noticed everyone in the cabin was asleep, except the fear-filled lady wife, who was looking over the back of her seat at Felix, shaking and trembling with a low, almost inaudible whiny turbo tone, "ooooooooooouuuuuuuu-wwwwww," her husband knocked out on three Seconal.

"Wow," Felix would remember, "and I thought that I was a bad flyer."

Felix loved telling stories, and that was a funny story to me, as it was to Felix, who laughed the whole time he was telling it.

In a hotel in Las Vegas during an informmercial convention, Felix mentioned that he didn't have a sense of humor until he was nine years old. He didn't know what humor was. There was laughter, but the idea of creating a joke or the telling of a joke was lost on him.

He said, "When I was younger, I didn't go to public school until I was, like, nine years old, and the kids at school were brought up knowing all these kid jokes, and I would be completely ignorant of what they were talking about. This was mostly because for a long time we lived on a desert island and had no references for humor. Simple things I found funny, but not jokes. I couldn't understand jokes. When a joke would come to the punch line, I would shake my head, and walk away. My parents never suggested that I have any other reaction than that. My parents also didn't tell jokes. So I never heard any until around nine. So at nine I slowly started to understand what other kids were laughing at."

I thought this was so sweet about Felix, and perhaps

would make an interesting movie. *The Boy Who Didn't Have a Laugh,* or something like that.

He also had a problem with his smile. Or his lack of a smile. For an informmercial presenter, to not have a smile was a debilitating thing. But somehow his energy made up for it. He couldn't execute the all-important "Bite and Smile" when selling a food product. So he just stayed away from food products, or he would do something else, like "Bite and Raise Eyebrows." He could get by because he was magnetic. He was like a little Elvis. And he could play a guitar too. He could hold down an audience of adults by the time that he was seven, playing his guitar and talking to the crowd.

When he died I found myself searching for a way to make sense of it. So I tried thinking like this . . . Suppose Felix and I attend a party together and Felix begins talking to a girl in one corner of the room while I strike up a conversation with some old friends in another corner about a new CPR Land bill that is trying to pass through Congress. Felix seems to be having a good time talking to this girl. He walks over to me and whispers in my ear that he is going to leave with the girl and will see me later. I stay at the party, I don't panic or anything, because I will see Felix later, I wasn't talking with him anyway, I am with my old friends talking about food production. I will see him the next day, or maybe the next week, but I am going to stick around the party until whenever it is that I decide to go. It could be a couple of more years, maybe thirty or forty. I will catch up with Felix later, right? We're all leaving the party, only he

left early. And when we leave the party, we'll have someone to go see. There is some reason that he has been
taken away so suddenly, and I guess it's that he has to go
on an adventure somewhere.

When I talked to him last it was over the phone. I
ended the conversation by saying, "See you later."

And Felix answered, "Who can tell? . . ."

♣

Jack is reminding me of Felix Arroyo more and more.
Jack wants to be a filmmaker. Felix had wanted to become a filmmaker, and get out of the teen presentation
business. Felix was a teenaged spokesperson, even
though he was twenty-two. A presenter for teens who
was not a teen himself. He was a teen at one time. However; time flies.

At least he wasn't a forty-something "teen." Maybe
that is what did him in. The prospect of becoming a teen
informmercial spokesmodel forever.

I would like to teach Jack some things about the
commercial film world, the things that I never got to
show Felix. Because of the benevolent intentions of
Jack's film work, and the relative amateuristic results, I
think of Jack as someone to foster, take under my wing.

I don't know what I can teach him. Little things perhaps. I can show him how to rent a stage and folding
chairs to prepare an informmercial.

I can encourage him in his lunacy. He's already a
lunatic. He is. His lunacy is why I am constantly in con-

tact with him. I am drawn to that. That, and because it looks like someone went to a Xerox machine before Felix died, and made a copy of him.

I sometimes suspect Jack is wanted by the police, and is perhaps the reason he is living here in Sasquatch, and not Texas where he came from. I'm afraid of that.

There are secrets all around Jack and Matt. They only go by first names. I don't know where they live. Spike does, though.

I tell Jack and Matt that I am writing a project about them. Well, not about them, but characters that resemble them. I want to ask them questions for this project I am making. But it is not a commercial. I don't know. A documentary screenplay? I tell them that I really don't know what I'm doing, but I am doing something with alarming compulsion and it has to do with them. Or characters like them.

They say, "Okay, you can ask questions," because they are kind, and because they don't mind humoring me—or whoever comes to them saying something like, "I don't know what I'm doing but will you help me do it?" Because they are young. They are still positive about things, unlike me. They have time. Time I don't necessarily have. I am running out of time.

I ask Jack if I can come to his film set where he is

filming *Don't Leave Me Georgetown*. He tells me that I cannot come to the set, but I go anyway.

Jack says his film is about the future.

I have a hard time finding out where Jack's planning to shoot the future. I cannot find his film set, because Jack hasn't told me where it is. But I hear from Spike, who is appearing in the film, that they are shooting in Jack's basement in north Sasquatch.

Let me tell you about Spike, since I keep mentioning him. He is an actor that I have used on a number of informmercial projects, or filmmercials, as I like to call them. Most of them have appeared on local cable television, to our credit. This was before I became older, before I had gone bankrupt, and became impure. Spike has had what you would think might be an exciting life although he has been damaged by it. He was a clown professionally in Las Vegas for a period of time. He was a kid clown that they threw around in a tumbling clown act at Circus-Circus, a casino in Las Vegas. He does tricks. He is used to taking incredible falls because of this training.

I think that he has a problem in that he is attracted to situations where he is likely to fall down and bruise himself. Miraculously he never gets hurt. He is falling in front of Jack's camera on the set of *Georgetown*. Falling for Jack with no insurance.

Jack cast Spike after meeting him in downtown Sasquatch. Spike was wearing a floor-length black-and-orange-striped coat and juggling batons that he had set ablaze. It is one of the many tricks Jack wants to adapt into his film project.

I look around the set. How disorganized it is. It's wonderful. Perfectly normal for low-budget filmmaking. Jack is of course doing all of the work. The others are standing around. Delegation problem.

There is a problem with the police uniform. Typical. No badge and no gun.

This is a great thing.

I leave before they begin to turn to me to complain. Because I am the only one not dressed like a slacker or a hippie, everyone seems to think I am in charge or can do something to correct things. It's not my fault. This is bad. Even for a student film. But Jack is learning. He needs someone to take care of him. Last week he canceled a shoot because his actor told him that he didn't feel like getting out of bed that day.

"The trials of low-budget filmmaking," Jack said.

I remember what it was like. It was hell.

I watch as Jack takes off to do a dangerous car shot with no insurance, disappearing into the city of Sasquatch.

When Jack returns, he has run out of film and waits a long time for the camera to be reloaded. He asks me about Sasquatch as if he is growing fond of it and needs more information. I look around.

I say, "It still feels like a small town. It is still the kind of town where people wave to each other from their car and yell to you as you are walking down the street. Hopefully good things," I say, "but not always. It's fifty-fifty nowadays. You have to take the good with the bad, Jack.

"Sasquatch is a town where everyone knows everyone else. Like you, me, Spike and Matt . . . Jack.

"To the north and to the south of Sasquatch, there are twelve-thousand-foot white-tipped volcanoes. Although one has blown its top recently. By recently, I mean within the last twenty years. Which is apparently very recent in volcano time.

"There are a couple of river valleys that run beside the volcanoes, and a lot is growing in the valleys because most of the time it is raining.

"One very exciting thing we have to look forward to in Sasquatch is that every three hundred years the tectonic plate here shifts, and a huge tidal wave floods the valleys with sea water. But I haven't seen that happen lately."

Dear Brutha,

 Hey, I'm workin' on my film for school. It's a gas, you'd like it, but I get hung up on the camera and forget about the other details, like buying film and shit. Matt's gonna be in the movie, and there's this crazy kid who can juggle named Spike, he's gonna be in da movie too.

We are gaining the confidence of that guy in da coat, the infomercial guy.

What a load.

We're becoming friends and he wants to help show us how to make the movie but he don't know how eitha, he makes infomercials, I don't wanna do anything like that shit.

Matt and I tripped around the cosmic block, that was lately, and we know how to use the comedy routines as an en-veloper.[21] We told ya about the comedy, I hope you don't mind, it helps us focus when we travel, and the vaudeville is as close to rock and roll which we used to use, you unda-stand. So far we ended up missin' the dimensional road cones by about twelve years, had to do it over again, we gettin' good though, you wait we might get our dimensional driver's licenses yet.

We got one little errand to run up in Stubtown, da fuzz is thinkin' that Blackie offed Matt's doppelganger Blake, and he

---

[21] An enveloper is Pink terminology for something that encases the focus of the future travelers, so that they are all concentrat-ing on the same thing at the same time. When the focus is total, then it allows the travelers to slip in between a moment in time and enter the dimensional level $Pink_1$. There are further dimen-sional levels: $Pink_2$, $Pink_3$, $Pink_4$, on up to $Pink_6$. Beyond the Pink dimension there is no more reality. But there is something beyond that the operators of Pink do not understand. The Pink travelers call this Dimension 7 and other than using it as a waste dump, they do not go there.

wants to fix dat up, make it betta so she don't have ta take the heat for somethin' he done. We're gonna fix it up. Give us some practice with the different levels and so on, Brutha.

All for now, over and out and all that kinda shit.

peace and love, Jack

♠

Pink

I am sitting in the Rubber Neck Grill one morning on a red leatherette and chrome stool, one that I can swivel around on to face a short-order counter. The morning temperature is promising us a hot day. Although, weather-wise, promises are often broken in Sasquatch. On my way in I could smell the wet cement sidewalk as store owners sprayed it down with hoses.

A rotund man named Harris[22] sits down next to me and gazes out the large plate-glass window . . .

---

[22] Harris' eyes are very dark, almost Middle Eastern. His legs and arms are short, and because of this he is all the time grabbing for things that are near his grasp, or kicking at things that are near his feet. He is Spunky's commercial-making peer, a person whom Spunky knows by trade mostly, who is always full of conversation when they run into each other. Harris is obsessively interested in image, and situation. He talks about his childhood reveries, DA haircuts in high school, cherry bombs blowing off at the end of football games and the like. He has gained a considerable amount of weight since his high school days, so now he is almost completely round. His voice is raspy and you would swear that his father was a Mafia don, or knew one really well. He blows out his words fast like they are coming out of a turbo, or spinning in a wind tunnel. He is amusing because of his disregard for little formalities in life, and his high regard for life's more intellectual possibilities. He took three months to name his daughter, Betsy, because Harris and his wife were so baffled by the

"In town for the long haul?" a woman behind the counter named Jolene Ricabaugh asks Harris.

Jolene[23] daylights as a waitress at the Rubber Neck.

Harris is a creature. I am a creature too. Jolene looks us two creatures in the eye as she places a menu in front of Harris.

"Jolene, imagine . . ." Harris says, "just imagine . . ."

"Whenever you say that, Harris," Jolene interrupts, imagining and chewing gum at the same time, "I know I'm in for a doozy."

Harris tries to hide a mischievous smile, then continues, obsessing busily.

"Just imagine . . . heaven, as if it's on the top of our heads, not in the sky or in the clouds as popular myth might have us thinking but *inside* our heads as if it is a large collective consciousness. Which it is."

"It's a collective up there, but it's collectin' dust is what it's collectin'," Jolene comments quickly, and in a no-nonsense manner slaps down a menu and snaps her gum.

---

metaphorical value and implication of a name. Harris is a nice man.

[23] Jolene Ricabaugh is usually the bartender or waitress at the Cinema Tavern, but during the school season, she daylights here. She has a large beehive hairdo that towers above her in a puffy soufflé, a soufflé which twists on her head this way and that as she talks or gestures. Her hair is bright red and she has one tooth missing on the right side. When things get out of control she can whistle through her missing tooth, commanding the toughest rabble-rouser to stop in his tracks.

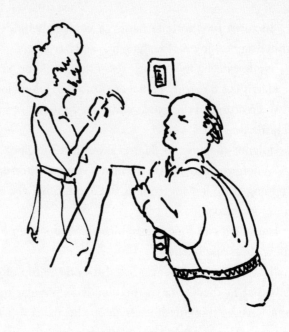

Harris and Jolene Ricabaugh

Harris glances at Jolene wondering if she's finished with her thorny waitress shtick . . . Jolene patiently nods yes.

Harris continues in short breathy bursts, "Our thinking mind is somewhere above and behind our eyes, up here on top"—Harris is patting the top of his head—"on the top part of our body. The thinking mind represents heaven. Like heaven, it gets a good rap. It is perceived as a good thing. An innocent thing, although some other parts of the body may disagree.

"The thinking mind has awarded itself this good reputation. The mind has decided for itself that it is the single most significant organ that mankind possesses and that it is the one great thing that separates mankind from the rest of the living creatures.

"The mind refuses to see any defective characteristics it may have that may burden mankind and it can outthink the other parts of the body."

Harris pauses, about to correct himself, then commits, "Yes . . . let's say it can outthink the other parts."

Heaven and Hell

"Okay . . ." Jolene says, "let's say that."

Jolene out of the corner of her eye can see a customer who is running low on coffee.

"Then there's below"—Harris' eyebrows raise—"our

sexual parts." Harris grabs his crotch with some intensity. This makes Jolene smile. I wonder how well the two of them know each other.

Harris' voice lowers a good octave, causing the other customers in the grill to turn their heads, wondering where the freak-show voice is coming from,

"And that's below heaven or the thinking mind which is up here"—patting the top of his head again—"on the top of the head.

"Below the earth's surface, which you could say is our eyesight, we have a symbolic hell. Hell is invisible. Hell is hiding underneath our clothing. Hell is down here where my little hand is." Harris' hands are little.[24]

"Jealousy is hiding under here too. And bad things. Divisiveness. Deviousness. Satan. This area of the body corrupts the other areas of the body with its desires, according to the mind/heaven."

Harris relaxes and sucks in air from the apparent effort of lowering his voice so much.

The curious and startled customers standing in the wings and sitting in booths turn back around to read their daily papers; having heard enough about heaven and hell for today, they are now ready to catch up on the dirt.

[24] Walt, who is another regular at the Rubber Neck Grill, says that all mass murderers have tiny hands, and Spunky begins to wonder about this as Harris lectures.

"So, I'm looking at heaven and hell as a concept that lives right within everyone of our physical bodies, rather than being something outside of us, like above the sky, or below the ground. A concept that is integral to our visual and physical perception and so subjective it becomes arbitrary, don't you think?" Harris declares.

"That's an interesting little notion, Harris," Jolene, entertaining Harris, says, lifting her ever-present order pad and pulling a pencil out of her beehive hair. "Can I take your order now?"

"Yes, ah . . . one obsessive and morally corrupt impulse, please."

"The regular?"

"And a side of bacon . . ." Harris says this as he taps the counter edge with two fingers from each tiny hand attempting to play the rhythm of a 1962 Surf-pop tune I think I can identify as "Wipeout," a rhythm I used to be able to tap.

This is the sort of daily entertainment that one might expect at a morning breakfast eatery like this. An ordinary day in an ordinary place like the Rubber Neck Grill in Sasquatch, Oregon.

I suppose that we like it here, squishy and wet as it is.

I say hi to Harris, and we start talking about loose ends. Business stories about this and that which wouldn't interest anyone. It hardly interests us. Our cellular phones touch on the countertop. I tell Harris that I have had two visions. It is time to share our visions.

"One vision I have had recently was under the influence of nitrous oxide inhaled while sitting in the dentist's chair during a tooth pull," I say. "This vision concerns Identity.

"The nitrous went in, and slowly I was surrounded by two nurses and a doctor of different races, social backgrounds, sexualities and sexual identities probably, as everyone has their own. I came to a conclusion that we are all the same person, only in different time continuums. The same creature. And the sameness applies not only to people but also to plants, dogs, birds and everything out here. They are the same as well. The same being, existing at the same time in many different places and on many different levels.

"By 'the same' I mean in the way that muscles which are used by a variety of different creatures are made of the same fibers, or, in the end, living cells are designed by nature so they look and behave virtually the same way, or, on another level, molecules are visually the same but they have different numbers of neutrons and protons and electrons.

"We have our consciousness; a bird has a consciousness that I, while under the influence of this nitrous gas, am inclined to think is similar to our consciousness. Consciousness being a tool, like a muscle. But consciousness, and thought, and premeditated thought are only tools. Thought is not the desired end-all objective of why we are on earth.

"The objective of why we are on earth, I believe, is

to try and stay alive. The thinking mind is a survival mechanism that humans and animals use to strategize, and to help get away from whatever is chasing them, or chase whatever it is they need to get ahold of in order to stay alive. It is an ordinary survival mechanism or tool. Like arms or legs."

Harris listens quietly and chews on a thick piece of bacon. Harris takes these thoughts seriously, although I am not sure that I do, because my mind has made the thoughts up and I don't trust my mind.

"Problem is," I continue, "and this relates to your vision a second ago, Harris; the problem is humans have a large enough brain they outsmart the rats and donkeys and dominate the earth; and the humans, being ever hopeful, think this is leading somewhere (toward a deity, for instance) when it only means that they have enough brains to dominate. They can outsmart the rats and donkeys of the earth but ultimately they outsmart themselves, by thinking that the brain, and thought, have a significance beyond the other senses, like, for instance, smell.

"Smell has its own language, and because humans don't revel in smell, they tend to ignore its significance. God may be a smell . . ."

I was stoned on nitrous oxide at the time. But even so.

Harris is still with me. Without commitment. That is how we review our visions, with no commitment. We come back at each other with more vision.

I tell Harris about a second vision that came over me during a later visit to the dentist. This other vision concerns Culture. And it is an innocent realization that human culture is a process that is simply allowed to develop as long as something doesn't show up (Conquistadors, Mongolians, Berserkers, Inquisitors, AIDS) to stop the culture dead in its tracks. It was another vision that contemplated survival.

"Even the most developed cultures eventually run into something that is hostile enough that it stops the culture cold in its tracks. The hostile force destroys the given culture enough that we, as descendants, can't figure out the most ordinary thing about the erased culture. As soon as the next thing comes along (cyborgs? viruses?) we will be dead meat, forget about it. And nobody will ever know what happened to us. Because it isn't really happening, other than what you see, smell, hear, taste, feel or think. What is really happening you can't experience. But sometimes you can."

I was getting further and further out.

Harris takes a sip of his orange juice and starts to mull this vision over for a second, and then he begins to respond to my culture vision that came to me in the dentist's chair by telling me about a film that he saw recently.

"It is about a superhero convention, and all the superheroes have to stand in long lines to enter this convention that is being held in a large stadium-sized barn." His eyes begin to mist up!

"They sleep in expansive bunk rooms, and they all sleep together, thousands of them, and they are all called Nemo," Harris says.

I open my mouth to speak, and then stop. He tells me a young student had brought the film over to his studio. His name was Jack.

(?)

♣

It is about this time that I hear of two Evangelists in the area who are talking about "rapturing." They are known simply as the Two.

People, I don't really know specifically who, are selling their houses and property in anticipation of a rapture. Or the Rapture. I don't know which. Is there supposed to be more than one? We all do it separately, I assume (but at the same time?).

If this is going to happen I don't exactly want to be left out, I would like to be part of it, rather than staying behind on the planet. If the Two are serious about it.

I heard from another, very reliable source that the Two are not Evangelists, but are from Los Angeles. Someone had mixed that up. Makes it a little less official, I would say. But only a little. Because I like Los Angeles, unlike other folks here in Sasquatch who feel they are being invaded by Angelenos. The earthquakes are shaking the Angelenos up here. We have them every-

where. They are at your door. They are in my trees[25] (ha-
ha).

Maybe the Two are running some sort of bunco ring.
I would like to meet these two who are known as the
Two.

※

---

[25] Spunky is referring to tabloid news camera crews and journalists from Los Angeles who wait outside his house and focus telephoto lenses at his windows in an effort to gather some tidbit of
information about what happened during the filming of *101 Useful Things You Can Do with Flamex,* a successful informmercial
that Felix Arroyo appeared in shortly before his death.

He couldn't handle the rock star idolatry, apparently, and Blake couldn't handle the up-close attention from all the marketing ploys dreamed up by his CD-spitting record company, Kangaroo Bulldozer Records.[26]

A lot of what he couldn't handle was the business, we know now, but at the time, it seemed to him, to Blake, that there was no more space left for himself. He had somehow very neatly co-opted all the space around him, beginning with his music, then his time. His immediate space was co-opted when he decided to get married and have triplets.

"Triplets? You're more like a damned cat than a rock star wife," Blake had commented in one of his more surly moods.

So now with triplets and the wife there was no space left, and he was the type of person who needed quite a lot of space as it turned out. He didn't think of himself as a person who needed any

---

[26] Kangaroo Bulldozer had arrived at that name because of the backgrounds of the partners in the company; one was from Australia and the other had backing from a construction company. One of the reasons Blake had signed with this independent record company was that he was fond of bulldozers, and he was attracted to the name.

space at all, but as he grew in stature, he needed more space.

Blake's physical presence reminded one of a little boy. He had a bowl haircut of blond hair. A small amount of post-adolescent acne, well, that was almost required in his line of work. And a voice that shot up the spines of all Middle America. He weighed only one hundred pounds, but you couldn't see this on a stage. He looked like Paul Bunyan up there.

His wife, Blackie, almost twice Blake's size, had a curious effect on the situation. Although she made Blake into a great straight man, she was getting in the way. She was interfering in what used to be Blake's private world. He had let her in, now she wasn't going to leave. And she wanted him to take a summer job that was going to net him three million dollars. Money that she thought that she had a right to. Money that could keep their little sons Bill, Binky and Bartholomew in private schools their entire lives, if going to private school their entire lives was something that the triplets wanted to do.

Blake's domestic situation had grown to resemble a nightmarish episode of *I Love Lucy.* Blackie came home one night, and positioned herself in the living room near the mantelpiece above a gas fireplace with small bundles of tied-up twigs in it. She looked above the mantel at the many colorfully painted dolls which she and Blake had composited into a freakish surrealist still life, then looked back across the living room at Blake, who was sitting in a green high-backed chair reading an equipment manual.

"I wanna have the curtains in this room done, Blake."

"Huh?"

"What do you think about black? You know, Toulouse-Lautrec had black satin curtains in his whorehouse bedroom in the upstairs of the Moulin Rouge. I want Lautrec whorehouse curtains, Blake. Are you going to get 'em for me or do I have to go out and get 'em myself, you pantywaist."

"Hey, fuck you."

Blackie smiled. "Okay . . ."

Normally, Blake would have been right there with Blackie, getting out the historic interior decorating books that showed the exact curtains one would expect to see in the Moulin Rouge. But this time he wanted to escape. To get away. From her. From his family. Run away from his responsibilities. Run away from the relatively good things in life and into the arms of a curious shopping habit.[27]

[27] This morning already, Blake had ordered two front-shovel Excavators built by Caterpillar with custom extras that increased the bucket-fill factor. These two purchases alone ran into the hundreds of thousands of dollars. And he had little land to excavate. There was always the farm. And in his seemingly directionless ac-

He didn't want to go off with Blackie on a hairy tear to find curtains to put in the fucked-up apartment that they had been renting. He wanted to buy a couple more tractors. And when Blackie realized that her man wasn't into interior decorating, then she lowered the hatchet.

"Blake, you no-good lousy rock and roll bum, get me some black satin curtains," she had said first. But she was only kidding. She walked across the living room of their rented Orlando apartment and picked up the two-inch-thick performance manual Blake was reading that was made by a name brand heavy equipment company.

"What are you going to do with all those bulldozers?" Blackie said.

"They aren't just bulldozers, they are all kinds of things," Blake said.

"They look like bulldozers to me, Blake."

"Yeah, I know. You should read more of these manuals, you'd get to know the difference," Blake said with a puff of underrated laughter.

"Well, what do you do with them?"

"I shine 'em up. Gonna build me a big old road with 'em, baby."

"Uh-huh. All right, well, I'm not into roads, I'm going to the store to buy some curtains. I'll be back in a little bit. Don't you go anywhere."

---

tivity, he planned secretly to build a road. A road that would lead him out of there, as in "I'm outa here."

The door closed behind Blackie, and Blake opened up his performance manual again.

Blake waited a long time for Blackie to return. He didn't go anywhere. The hours stretched into days and the days into weeks, when finally Blake realized Blackie wasn't coming back. He hadn't seen his triplets either.

Blackie had taken little Bill, Binky and Bartholomew away and started living in a hotel in Fiji with that loathsome rocker—Tony T.—who was bending the popularity curve in his direction by the minute, and who Blake began to suspect was acting as Blackie's surrogate lover. Not only that, but Tony, who was climbing the charts a little too fast for Blake's comfort, was building a little guesthouse for Blackie and the triplets on his Montana ranch.

Blake knew for a fact Tony T. was not as talented as he himself was. But there was evidence of Tony T.'s album rising steadily up the charts, and Blake's wife and kids had gone off to live with the dude. It was right out of a rock and roll Western.

Tony had been circling the globe generating international press as his album slowly picked up in sales. He hailed from Louisville, and his father was an old blues fill-in man, which is where Tony learned his snaky hooks in the middle of his songs. He had a head and face that looked like a classic cartoon man-after-explosion, hair that shot back and black stuff on the nose, mouth and cheeks, a sort of stylized rocker makeup that irritated Blake.

Blake had a chance to look back on these separate realities while his plane to Stubtown taxied down the runway of the Orlando airport.

"Magazine, sir?" the stewardess asked Blake as he slumped in his first-class seat.

Blake just looked at her like, "Why don't you like me?"—not really realizing that it wasn't Blackie that was offering him the magazine.

This really worried the stewardess, who had somewhat of an inferiority complex. She placed the magazine down next to him and hustled down the aisle, occasionally looking back over her shoulder at Blake.

Well, now, it wouldn't be long before we were in the air . . . Blake thought. But one thing worried him. Would anyone be at the Lotus Hotel when he arrived in Stubtown? He'd wanted to check, but he didn't have the telephone number on him. The Lotus had a permanent guest through whom Blake could score mid-to-heavy farm machinery and fork-lifts at wholesale prices.

Call Li'l Chub, he'll have the number. Use the Air-Phone.

Buzz/Click. Dial. Ring. "Hello?"

"Hello, Li'l Chub? 'S Blake."

"Blakey honey, what-up? Hey, I was just going through Caterpillar's twenty-fifth edition handbook, hey . . . have you checked out these articulated trucks? I mean, damn, Blake, some models can climb a thirteen percent grade at fourteen miles an hour in second gear with a fifty percent payload!! 'Least that's what the performance specs indicate."

"Yowee. But in that edition I was particularly taken with the specs on that D5C series 111 Bulldozer and those special 'Dozing Tools that come along with it. Man!"

"Oh, hey, yeah."

"You have the L's number, don't you?"

"What, you comin' up here? When?"

" 'S like ten-thirty."

"I'll be sure L is around and that we can get ahold of as many vehicles as we want and I will pick you up. Okay?"

"Good. S'ya then."

Click. Buzz. Whissshhh.

Now we're talkin', Blake thought, and picked up the magazine that the stewardess had left on the seat next to him. "Holy fuck!" Blake said out loud as he stared at the front page of *Movers and Graders* magazine.

Who could have left this here? Blake forgetfully wondered to himself.

♣

Outside my home, my little home on the hill next to the trees, there is an innocent plot of grass that runs the length of the curb beside the road. It is only twelve inches wide at the most and curved, for I live on a curve. I say that this grass is innocent as if I know, I assume its innocence. At least it is innocent enough that the cars have no claim on the grass. But it is nevertheless subject to a kind of bullying from the cars that run across it every now and again in their attempt to destroy it. I see a long tire track that runs the entire corner of the property, a dark and muddy rut that is most distasteful. Someone is having fun with the grass (or with me). But I don't know who it is. I never see it happening.

The grass hasn't done anything about it except slowly grow back. Teenagers no doubt are torturing the grass strip. Because they have nothing else to torture. J-D[28] thinks that it is funny and the teenagers are only having fun. He would think that way with a name like

---

[28] J-D is a disc jockey by trade and an import from Holland. He is the one person in Sasquatch that Spunky has remained in contact with over the past twenty years on a relatively regular basis. He is large, by shape, and resembles a Dutch Biker. He has a great beard, which resembles those on the men decorating Dutch Masters cigar boxes. J-D's morals and sentiments do not necessarily match up with those that are common in North America, which can lead to interesting and comic situations. Which is why he

J-D. Innocent fun, he thinks. Maybe they are more van-dalistic in Holland than I had realized.

When a few weeks go by and the grass begins to grow back and repair itself, and it looks like it might make it, then the teenagers drive over it again, and gouge it out with their black-and-brown tire tracks. And my heart sinks. Am I being materialistic? Overprotective? It is as if civilization were trying metaphorically to stamp out the last strip of nature in an all-concrete city.

I occasionally conspire to place nails in the grass, for the teenage tires. But then I fear even harsher retalia-tion. My house is made of wood. Maybe there are wooden matches where those rubber tires come from. Maybe they are Dutch teenagers. I ignore it, or I try to. And the curb of grass tries to grow back.

✦

The phone rings. It's for Jack. I ask the person on the other end of the line, "Jack who?" They don't know Jack's last name. I realize that I don't know his last name either. I insist they tell me Jack's last name, but they decide they have a wrong number.

"My number isn't wrong," I say.

I hang up the phone and climb the stairs to my ply-wood-paneled attic retreat to work on the fantasy action story that I write in my spare time.

---

thinks that it is good fun when the teenagers drive over people's lawns.

My story, which I am planning to adapt into a screenplay, was once called $ THE MONEY SHOT $.[29] But I have changed the title to $-GREAT SKULL ZERO-$. It is written with a traditional three-act Hollywood structure that I have allowed to guide my style after taking a one-day-long screenplay-writing seminar. The Saturday seminar that Steve,[30] Joanna[31] and I took

[29] This title has only a surface relationship to the term "the money shot," which is used to describe where the money is being spent on the production side, or the reason that the audience is going to see your production. If, for instance, you use a high-paid actor in your commercial or your film, you refer to the close-up on the expensive actor's face as "the money shot." If you are talking about a porno film, the money shot might be the same as the cum shot, a reason that many of the viewers are spending their money on it.

[30] Steve is a very quiet young filmmaker. He met Spunky at a potluck over Labor Day about four years ago. Steve and Spunky actually carried on a relationship for a year but eventually they broke it off. Steve has red hair and wears it short, rarely speaks, prefers to answer questions, and usually dresses in a suit. He has written a lot of articles for a film quarterly that is printed up in Slabtown, Washington, and does his best to support the activities promoting Lesbian and Gay equality.

[31] Joanna is an animator in Sasquatch of some renown. She is currently working on a short animated film called *Someone Watches over Me*. She is pretty and wears fashionable sunglasses that are prescription. She is methodical and practical in her speech and is liked by the other filmmakers in town. As a medium, film suits her.

together was where we learned about film structure, pacing, story and dialogue; everything we needed to know to conform to the Hollywood norm.

At this point in my filmmaking career I am trying to conform, mostly because all other efforts at writing engaging, original and sellable screenplays have failed. I gave up trying to be the rebel I thought that I was when it was fashionable to be a rebel. Nowadays it is fashionable to give up and conform. So I gave up, and I'm trying to conform and sell out.

I click on the keys of my old IBM electric typewriter, constructing the simple story set on a remote island in the midst of a jungle war where creatures are devouring each other in their search for insane intelligence.

The circus tent looks orange-gray in the island twilight. The hollow wooden tiki sentries at the four corners of the quadrangle silently hum, animistic voyeurs, surveillance idols. The day has moved in, squatted in a shocked blue, becoming an almost sexual horizontality of awakening clouds and blown away by night's onslaught of black carapace and moon madness. In fact, the lupine night is a black beaver-hair top hat, a resonant article of universe, an object of secret dreams and the cruel theater of flesh.

On our island circus a ringleader is kin to shaman and we need one, wearing panther tuxedo, green face paint and beads of glowing purple resin, eyes glowing hyena red from behind a gentleman's mask, gloves gone neon in the river of time. Roentgen paused at the tent flap feeling for a cigar at an inside pocket, reaching for the remote control to raise the perimeter laser barrier. It often reminds him of a blank musical notation when the red lines leap across space, perhaps to be filled with the notes of confused animals, human or otherwise, making random compositions with their screams when they accidentally stumble through. The tiki scans the jungle with infrared video. The night drums begin. Roentgen lowers himself through the jaws

of the stone naga that serves as portal in the
quadrangle into the tunnel below . . .

Giant glowing tadpoles swim in an irides-

Roentgen

cent lagoon surrounded by concrete palm trees
and a ruined populux sleep-casket hive looking
much like Frank Lloyd Wright gone wrong on
Tupperware. Out on the kaleidoscopic waters,
out on the purple mists, a black rubber canoe
with green light shooting up into the sky from
the floor through the jumbled leg shadows
of cloaked figures approaches silently like a
ghostly image from the mind of Böcklin. They
approach a jetty of animal skulls reaching out
from a plaza where folding chairs covered in
Spanish moss are arranged around a fancy din-

ner table replete with an ice penis sculpture. Here sit Baccara Nascimento and Fedorco Quamochi. Baccara is reading an old stained newspaper and drinking a martini to candlelight. Fedorca is quietly napping with a lemur in his lap also napping. They are both naked but smeared with neon-green insect repellent. As the boat arrives, Baccara throws his martini in Fedorca's angelic face, waking him and the monkey in a squall of grunts, farts and squeaks. "The Boys are here, Dorko . . . get the tequila and limes . . ." Suddenly a giant of a Negress steps out of the shadows and puts a spear to Fedorco's chest. "The good tequeya, Dorko, you bastardo." "Darling, I didn't see you. Isn't it a wonderful evening?" "No, Baccara, it's not, all my panther traps are empty, and what's worse, the slave I've been tracking all day has eluded me." "I'm sorry, dear, perhaps a drink." "Yes, perhaps . . ." The velvet-caped boys disembark with their parcels and hides and a small Oriental woman in her thirties, blindfolded, wrapped in green silk with a yellow bow tied around her face. "Here's your new slave, Yolandé Negrita." Fedorca passes out the . . .

I listen to the whirring of the electric typewriter motor as I pause from writing $-GREAT SKULL ZERO-$.

A car passes by my window with a busted muffler. A voice yells in the distance. A voice with a familiar quality to it. Like Jack's voice, or Felix's voice. Hmm.

I imagine Felix's sickly fluttering on the sidewalk outside the gambling joint Thundermountain. It is weird how the Felix feeling comes and goes. Some days are apparently normal, and other days I will begin to cry, unless I am already crying when I awake. Coming out of a crying dream, crying.

I am lost.

I realize that a lot of time has gone by and I haven't left the house since his death, except when I went to Las Vegas to direct my informmercial, and when I look for Jack or go to the Rubber Neck Grill. There is the phone, however, and I talk to many friends about Felix.

Journalists come to visit too, and there are journalists and photographers camped out in the trees outside my Victorian house overlooking Sasquatch. They sit high in the trees, peer in the second-story windows, and take a couple of pictures now and again. Waiting for something to happen. They are doing their job, I know. Sometimes I feel like talking to them, to make friends with them. I only hope that they write some good things and don't dwell too much on the bad things that surround Felix's disappearance. But of course they do. That is all they are writing, it seems. I suppose they are going to write whatever they want to. They need an angle. It is tedious.

I go outside and look up at the pine tree in front of my house.

"Hey!" I say.

An answer comes back. "Hey what?" a voice in the tree says, as if the tree were talking to me, John Muirishly.

I say, "Hey, your children must miss you right now." But they don't answer me.

"Remember the bullet train?" Sue[32] had said on the phone. I can still hear the train bumping over the tracks.

It took a moment to remember the time we were promoting our Flamex Compound informmercial. Riding on the bullet train, which was traveling at 120 miles per hour. All the young Japanese girls that swarmed around Felix with notes for him.

Notes that said, "I think you a nice person. I like meet you and your family." They loved him so much. They loved but they were not in love.

Elisabeth Kübler-Ross (I heard) wrote that we shouldn't despair, that when we die, we in effect don't die. It is hard for her to explain. It requires reading her book to get an idea of what she means. She made this

---

[32] Sue is Felix's old girlfriend. She has long blond hair and wears a beret a lot of the time. She, like Spike, works in a coffee shop, except the one that she works in is in San Francisco. She is a deep thinker, Spunky thinks, and she is actually onto something.

statement after decades of research about death and dying.

I wonder why she wrote that we don't die. Except maybe she means that we aren't alive either.

I need to ask Jack.

Jack says, "Life is like wadda, and as individuals we are like a dammed-up body of wadda. When we die the dam collapses and da body rejoins the rest of the waddas."

I receive a phone call from my Las Vegas production executive. The connection isn't that good, he is calling from a plane. He wants to tell me that he is really excited about the last informmercial project we made together for Kenny Sabene's autographed sabers. I know that he doesn't mean what he is saying, what he means is that it has scored well, and he wants to put in a call supporting the project before he gets caught not paying attention.

For a moment, a couple of junior executives also get on the line, they say, "We really believe in this project . . ." I want to ask them, "Really, really, really?" But I don't want to sound ungrateful. I am satisfied that I have made them happy. It makes me happy if they are happy. He says, "We are on the right track and if everything continues to go our way it'll be nothing but a really, really, smooth (sssssss)" . . . and then he is cut off by a loud hissing sound (sssssss). Which is startling at first, and is not that bad a metaphor for life itself. Life just starts to get going when it is abruptly cut off by a great hissing sound.

I changed when Felix left the picture. I did. Before he left, everything was the same, but now, everything is different. Now there is a hissing sound. There is an awareness of wasted unending events I have to pass through on our way to an end. Once, we had someone who was important to us. Now it wasn't like before; before he mysteriously disappeared.

Felix had been talking of aliens. I have to ask Jack about aliens. Or Nemos as he calls them. Hmm. I am getting a creepy feeling.

I have to ask Jack what his last name is.

We loved Felix so much. Felix always knew what to do when everyone else was at their end. He was a humanitarian. He always had the hope. He always had the power, and the glory. He always had the nice thing to say,

Felix

and whenever there was any trouble, he was the one to figure a way out of it. The only thing that made Felix frustrated was when he couldn't settle an argument between two people. He worried about arguments as if life depended on harmony. He gave us harmony.

Felix told me once that the aliens are really us. How did he know that?

He said, "They are us trying to reach us, and as

much as they want to talk and explain things to us, they can't. Or they won't. But when we adjust our attitudes enough and we finally figure out that they are around, then they will expose themselves to us. They will visit us. We will feel as if we are being Born Again. As if we are rapturing . . ."

Maybe that is what death is like . . . rapturing. I wonder where the Two are. I wonder what happened to the other two, Matt and Jack.

Dear Brutha,

How is you. I gotta tell you, Brutha, that we have been very pissed off at this Pink$_2$ project,[33] and that you have changed dimensions and work for a new racket. Whadda we do now?

There are going to be a lot of people lookin' for us now. And Matt spent all the money, mostly on heavy machinery, what a whack, he did buy some rock and roll equipment for a local band here, and we'll never get that back.

Anyway, with all respects, Brutha, we gonna try and

---

[33] Because of a restructuring at the top, Matt and Jack are up shit's creek without a paddle. They are worrying about a number of people whom they have led into the Pink who, because of the shake-up at the top, have turned into dimensional boat people looking for a level. Jack's also worried about the money that belonged to the missing dimensional travelers, most of which has been spent by Matt.

split now. But I gotta finish my film, or I'll be in even more shit.

Anyway, I promised myself to finish my film. It is almost done.

Well, I guess that we are on our own now. It's kinda scary, 'cause we don't know what we're doin'.

Oh, you gotta see these vaudeville routines, baby they are outa sight. Hope to catch up with you layta.

peace and love and all kindsa good shit, Jack

Πινκ αλτ. υνιϖερσ.

I am in a small bed, with a plastic pillow. I can stare out of a window four stories high in the middle of a large city. We cannot go outside. We cannot. The officers, or counselors, can. They come and go. But we remain. It is part of the therapy. There is one of us from down the hall named Lonnie. He stops for a moment at the open door of my room, the one that is to remain open all day until lights out. Lonnie says, Hi. He rights his inch-thick Medicare-issued black-framed broken-rimmed glasses on his nose so they are not crooked anymore. When he speaks, a curious Mickey Rourke strangled voice comes out, seeming to untie his sentences as he says them, slowly inspecting the meaning and syllables of each word as he is saying them, as they are dragging through his throat.

He says, Yeah, I saw, you, in the hallway, downstairs . . . and, wanted to, have, a discussion, with you about this place, to see what you think about . . . uh, whatever, yeah; later, we should talk, and, maybe, we can be friends . . .

I hadn't planned on making any friends while I was in here.

We are two of only four white people in the facility. All the others are black or Hispanic, which is nice. But it is a change. The blacks are nicer than the whites. More together. My two roommates are black. I feel black now. But I am not. I'm not. And I don't guess I ever will be.

We are here in this facility to talk, mostly about ourselves or each other, there being nothing else to talk about. One guy came into the facility recently and started to talk about the record business. And he was so busy talking about the record business that he didn't realize that I was in the business too. He was a record executive of some kind, and he was extremely busy talking about new bands and new records, and before you knew it (or before he knew it) he was on his way out the dreaded, or beckoning, downstairs door. He had some big deals to make on the outside, I guess. That is what happens to you if you don't talk about yourself or about others but instead talk about something like records. What happens when you talk about the outside is that you begin feeling you have no use for being here and you get up and you leave.

This is a Convention, of sorts. To find out how we work (to find out our superpowers). To find out about our mortal powers. As inmates, we are different, yet we are all the same. The thought of leaving through the front door of the building rests idly in each one of us. Some of us do not want to go outside the building because we are afraid of what is out there. Others

want to go outside the building but cannot go because
for them there is a choice of either spending time in
this mansion or spending time in jail.

Cloudy-Bright Center

I called it a mansion. It is an old mansion of sorts,
but it has been institutionalized. With cement floor-
ing, and gray fencing, and red exit doors and eleva-
tors. Only a little of the original mansion is visible.
There are supposedly ghosts in the mansion we are in.
It was built eighty years ago, when the city of Orlando
was much younger. It probably was a very social place.
I'll bet they drank bathtub gin here in the late twenties.

This place is called the Cloudy-Bright Rehabilitation Center. When I first got here, some tall guy
calling himself Tex, or was it Trax, sat next to me and
tried to explain their problem. They called themselves
a co-dependent, and in the conversation they told me

a rehab joke, "When a person with a 'co-dependent personality dies, somebody else's life flashes before his eyes," which made me nervous, especially since it seemed he was more interested in my problems than in his.

During the day if anything goes really wrong, one of the forty-odd patients usually ends up outside the building. And we never see them again, or hear from them, or really know what happened. It is as if they are banished to another world. A horrifying world. A world that doesn't work. It affects each one of us. If someone says, So-and-so left the building, it is an introduction to a complicated discussion between the members who are left inside the building. We talk about it all day long.

For instance, just yesterday, something that had been brewing for a long time came to a head. And the whole thing blew up in one of the group therapy sessions that we attend. (Group therapy is something that I find enjoyable, but with other patients there are problems. Lonnie feels that these group discussions have a lot to offer, but he gets nervous when he thinks that he is in a bogus group and is sitting with people who are lazy about trying to work the group, are too closed off with their emotions, or, as he puts it, simply don't give a fuck and won't try. It is even worse when he thinks that his counselor, who is running the group, is doing the same thing. Lonnie has changed his group three times now.) A young black man named Donald was telling his group this story about how one of his friends held down a cop and shot him in the head as he pleaded for his life. Lonnie was not ordinarily in my group session but this day he was. He stood up in the middle of the session and accused the counselor of manipulating Donald to the point where he was now endangering his safety by spilling this incriminating story. The counselor stands up and berates Lonnie for interrupting. The situation escalates into a physical challenge from the recovering-alcoholic counselor, sort of the "Come on, big boy, let's see what you got, this is gonna be fun . . ." variety, so Lonnie stands up and decks the guy while Donald sits in his chair smiling.

Then something new happens. We are scolded by the orderly. I hadn't noticed, but the intention of the orderly was in fact merciful. He was trying to keep us from getting in trouble. The guests are becoming comfortable and are betting on the scampering of the mice in the kitchen as if they are at a horse race. The group head puts a stop to this off-the-beaten-track betting. A little patient was trembling when she protested, but that is because she didn't know what was good for her. She was kicked in the rump.

We go about our business of communing, writing, thinking, smoking and making toast. Toast is a popular thing here. We are all passengers wandering through a fifty-one-room train. Only we cannot wander very far. We cannot leave. We cannot.

Lonnie is making himself comfortable. He has been through numerous programs before and he knows the ropes. Lonnie says, in the rehab stone age, before psychologists were making so much money off of Medicare, when a patient was reprimanded for not observing the rules, the patients were forced to take care of themselves. There were only addicts—no doctors. And the rules were a lot stricter. If a patient needed discipline, he was handed a broom and told to sweep a sunbeam on the floor until it was swept across the room and disappeared as the sun went down. It was a punishment called "sweeping the sun" that could take hours.

Lonnie isn't particularly interested in leaving this place because he has nowhere to go. When he came in he was homeless, and when he gets out he will be a homeless problem. Because of this he is constantly trying to get admitted into a shelter before it eventually comes time for him to be kicked out.

All of the counselors are in the same boat, they have a problem on the outside with their own dysfunctions. They are recovering. Recovering from life, essentially, is what we are coming to grips with. You appreciate how hard life is when you spend a little time in here with the others. It becomes harder when you are in here. That is, your perception of exactly how hard it is on the outside becomes far more elaborate and amplified when you are inside than when you are running around on the outside.

That could be one of the problems with running around on the outside. You don't see that you are actually in this whole freaky world. Inside, it is simple to see what the hell happens on the outside, and why we have to take it easy. How we have to learn that we have it made on the outside, most of us, and that we needn't let our emotional problems get the better of us. Or we amp out and drive ourselves to Edge City. Something like that.

It is complicated, and that is what we are attempting to learn. It is a lifelong exercise. And we will be exercising until we finally check out and disappear, or die, or whatever happens when you "leave the facility." This is an alternate universe that is calm and safe, and we are here to help each other.

♠

I t's interesting, the very quality that Swifty[34] has that makes it difficult for him to climb up to the great informmercial presentation delivery heights he is capable of, is the exact thing that makes him the super big star he has become: Trouble, with a capital T and that rhymes with P and that stands for Pain.

He's got pain. His self-image has been so decimated that at times he loses the confidence to pull off a simple performance. But his pain is the thing that makes people scream for more of him on the informmercial screen, the thing that makes him so attractive and comfortable. The audience seems to want that pain, above anything else.

As an informmercial director, I try to find people in

---

[34] Swifty has dark hair, a long lanky body. In Spunky's eyes Swifty has the perfect butt, a forlorn longish face with outstanding, knowing eyes that are black and reflect a lot of light. He is the enfant terrible, the boy-about-town, the athletic bungee jumper, and Spunky considers Swifty to be the best-looking human being north and south of the Tropicana Grill. Spunky is in love with him. Spunky calls him Swifty as a nickname. They are close, but they don't phone each other all the time, they used to have a thing going, now Spunky isn't sure. Spunky kind of misses him. Swifty moves in higher circles now, and also swiftly, thus Spunky's nickname . . .

pain to put in my commercials, because that is what sells the product in the end.

Pain is what works for the audience.

The barbecue with Matt, Jack and my gay friends has fallen through. There was a miscommunication. And this is the Fourth of July weekend. How inept. We must look like a bunch of old doddy wastrels to these stoner kids. We are getting nearer to that every day. A few more years and we'll be doddering enough.

I don't want to dodder. I fear that. I want time to stop so that I won't grow that way. But it just keeps coming.

J-D was planning a barbecue and didn't remind Chester about it, who doesn't listen to messages left on his machine by J-D anyway. That is because he goes on, I suppose.

The kids probably saw a boring old time coming in any case and wanted to steer clear of it. I told Jack that instead of a barbecue we were going to have dinner at a restaurant instead. He agreed at first, then he called back and said he was just going to "hang around." But he wanted to talk the next day about something . . . I wondered what it was.

I asked him about the film of Cowboy Nemo, I didn't know it was already a film . . .

Jack paused, then said, "We have to talk."

He says he will tell me about that, later. I'm afraid now.

I have offered Jack money to write. Maybe that is what he wants to talk about. Maybe Matt wants something too. Maybe he wants some new skis . . . ha-ha. Maybe he wants to write too. Good. Two writers. I need that. I need two writers in my employ, whatever comes into their maniacal heads, writing up a storm. That would be like heaven (?). We could hire readers then. We would be too busy to read what we were writing. I do have a perverse need to make an industrial production company in the image of a big company, like in Las Vegas. To play the game. Except on my own terms, with crazy daredevil stunt kid informmercial writers.

Oh, I want to meet Vegas on their own corrupt gridiron and play the home team with some kick-ass material that they'd never even see coming, and smoke them and show them how to sell a product. I know I can do that. And conquer the airwaves, like a renegade conqueror or a War Lord.[35]

---

[35] There was a time when Spunky wanted to say "fuck it all" and move to the Golden Triangle of Burma, Thailand and China and become a War Lord intern with some of the drug war lords familiar to that area. It was something that Danny Feldman and Spunky used to joke about, becoming War Lords, when they were working on sweetening (sweetening is a term used to describe the overlays and sound manipulations used to enhance the generally problematic sound of a game show or informmercial. This would include my favorite manipulation tool, the canned laughter machine) the soundtrack of some of their informmercials. Only after a while Spunky considered actually buying the one-way plane

Yes, a War Lord from the north who pillages the 1-800 numbers of the world. I am sure the competition is thinking the same thing. The competition works on their projects all day every day. It is such a competitive business.

Berserker/Mongolian/War Lord/Conquistador/Informmercial maker.

🌲

A filmmaker named Todd Truelove is visiting from Germany. I go to see his films and listen to him talk with Jack and Matt. J-D is also sitting with us.

Truelove stands in a crowded theater that is part of the Museum in downtown Sasquatch. The inside of the theater looks as if it was designed in the mid to late sixties. It still has that fifties Eisenhower look about it. The sound in the theater is horrible. All the walls are made of brick and so they reflect the sound in a kind of giant reverb box. This could be good for some performances, but not for film. Truelove's hair is curly and flies straight back from his sloped forehead, giving him a fast stream-

---

ticket to that other universe of war and pain and just staying over there. Hypothetically this was probably all right, but seeing as how Spunky is fifty-two, and he would be learning jungle combat from young soldiers who had been fighting since they were two years old, he could see how he might not have the slightest chance of working his way up the War Lord Ladder, and would certainly die by gunshot or landmine.

lined look. He wears a Polo shirt and tan chino pants, probably from the Gap. He looks healthy, and he is extremely assertive and positive about himself, his films and his theories and ideology.

He begins his talk with some didactic statements about the theoretical uses of film, but it mostly seems like his interest lies in the areas of death, pain, fear and stressfulness. Which has a ring to it that is uniquely German in my limited knowledge of the Germans and their culture.

Todd shows three films. One is an investigation of Kuwait after the Gulf War. Another is about a tribe of Mali men who dress as women, or what seems like a woman to us, to win their bride. Then another film has a removed and intense vision. A disturbing Truelove vision.

In a room, a young slightly overweight boy wearing a baby-blue cardigan pullover sweater with red stripes at the cuffs and the neck. He is also wearing dress pants. They have apparently dressed him up for some reason. Perhaps in anticipation of a visitation? He seems to be blind, and he is perhaps deaf. He makes embarrassing farting sounds with his mouth. These seem to be the only sounds he knows how to make. There is a small bed with an ocher bedspread with small flowers printed on it with more baby blue. The floor is tile. Red tile. We have all of our primary color groups right here within this vision. Blue, red and yellow ocher. Now, there also is a red ball with white spots on it. A white-spotted red ball about seven inches around. The boy finds it on the floor and holds it. Then violently he strikes it with his head. Then he hits his face with it, causing some pain, which he likes.

He sits dazed for a second. I don't know how I can tell that he is dazed, because he has no eyes. The eyes are altogether missing, which is why I think he is blind. They are not there at all. After he recovers from hitting himself hard with the ball, he lets the ball go and it bounces away, across the red tile floor.

Hands, I don't know whose, put a red-and-white radio in the blind boy's arms. It could be a rather stylish radio, if one were living in the 1930s. The radio has very simple rhythmic music playing from it. He feels the music, and holds the radio close to his chest, feeling the speaker. He tries to push the radio into his head, kind of like he did with the ball, but with less violent forcing of the radio into his head. He wants the music to be inside of his head. For some odd reason I have a brief thought of Matt and his music. I get the idea that music means a lot to Matt.

After the films, Truelove talks about other states of consciousness with the audience of about four hundred who have all stayed to hear him answer questions.

"I am trying to get at another level of consciousness with these films I have made. Film is, in itself, another dimension, another time, recorded and played back in a new dimension."

I notice after this statement, Jack and Matt take a

long look at each other as if they are thinking the same thought at the same time.

"I dismiss New Age thought," Truelove says. "I am not a New Ager, and I think that these people who are into crystals and these sorts of things are hypnotizing themselves, and walking around in a sort of permanent hypnotic trance and delusion. Even though my films often discuss altered states and sometimes reply to our questions about existence with references to cataclysmic or spiritual answers, I am not an advocate or a member of the New Age."

I notice Matt is visibly antagonized by this somewhat arrogant statement.

He also dismisses Cinema Verité, the harbinger of the French New Wave. Since the German cinema of the seventies (of which Todd is a member) took over from the French New Wave of the sixties perhaps there is a bit of territorial jealousy here. He elaborates on his opposing cinematic technique.

Truelove maintains he is looking for truth, but not the supposed truth of Cinema Verité (truth twenty-four frames a second?), but manipulated truth, which he thinks is more truthful than pointing a camera in different directions in the middle of a situation.

"With Cinema Verité, the cameraman is trying to grab whatever is passing senselessly through the air, like trying to catch little birds as they fly by, or the procession of a line of ants on the ground, little ants, which mean nothing," Truelove says, getting rather worked up over the concepts of Cinema Verité.

"Fucking German," J-D says under his breath. The Dutch have a well-founded hatred of the Germans because during World War II they burned down their city of Rotterdam, where J-D is from.

After the discussion and the showing of his films, the film center director invites a few people along for dinner. We go, and sit next to him in a dark wooden booth with low lighting, classical music playing and lots of wine going around. Jack and Matt get loaded up on the wine and gaze at the director sitting across from us at the heavy wooden table.

What Todd Truelove mainly discusses is truth in cinema. He avoids any direct debate about truth itself, and what real truth is, because he says that we could spend days on that subject, but he is an avid opponent of what he calls Cinema Verité. Matt's eyes get a challenging glaze in them when he hears Truelove's strength of conviction about Cinema Verité.

Truelove is a person who very definitely likes to argue. So is Matt.

J-D chose not to come to dinner with us because he feared that he would get into a big fight with the director over World War II.

J-D said, "The worst thing that I could say to Mr. Truelove is: Where is my bicycle!"

"What?" I asked.

"During World War II, after the Germans invaded Holland, they stole all the bicycles, so every kid in Holland had his bike stolen by the Germans," J-D said.

"Cinema Verité is a big joke, it is an irresponsible

way to handle the medium of film for anyone interested in any kind of truth," Truelove says to us in a kind of lecturing tone. "It bothers me that the technique is supposed to be used as a way to get at the truth. Because, in fact, it gets at nothing. It is only a meager and directionless pointing of the camera in a helpless attempt at capturing something, anything. There is so little control that it cannot reveal its own self-centered nonsense." During our discussion of truth, in the wooded restaurant, the German director says, "My intention when making a documentary film is to control the images in a way that allows the filmmaker to get at a more revelatory and transmissible truth."

It sounds New Age to me.

There is a discussion about Oliver Stone, for some reason.

"Oliver Stone has never made a good film," the German filmmaker says.

"*JFK,* what about *JFK?*" Matt says.

"It was a terrible film," Truelove says, "a complete middle-class fascination with these conspiracy theories. Oliver Stone's biggest crime is that he knows what he is doing. He is playing the audience for their sicknesses. This whole paranoia about the JFK assassination is just nonsense. And, you know, every person that I meet and discuss this assassination with has never even read the Warren Report. The main documented investigation into the assassination, they have never read this.

"I tell you, you have to read this document. It is a

wonderful piece of writing. It is a great piece of modern prose, it is so well constructed and so well written it made me cry when I read it. And I could not put it down. Eight hundred pages of brilliant prose. The middle class's preoccupation with these conspiracy theories is a modern sickness of the middle classes. And it is just nonsense."

"What is he talking about? *JFK* is a good movie," Matt says to Jack, defending Oliver Stone.

"I think *JFK* is a good film," Matt says to Truelove.

"No, you are fooling yourself, it is not a good film at all, I tell you, it is a complete distortion of the highest order," Truelove insists emphatically, putting his hands together in front of his face, as if he were putting together pieces of a puzzle. "It is a manipulation of the paranoia of the American middle class and their preoccupation with these conspiracies that never happened."

Matt has his gestures too. He has a way of getting into his thoughts as if he is typing them on a tiny typewriter that is sitting in front of his nose, as if he is pinpointing little truths that are appearing before his two eyes, one that gleams with red wine and the other with territorial challenge.

"The idea that the conspiracy is all made up is incredibly naive, Mr. Truelove," Matt says to him. "Oliver Stone makes populist films, but in *JFK* he is constructing an Aria around a wealth of lies and cover-ups and murders and conspiracies, and binds them together into one great attack on a postwar American Political-Industrial Complex which is bigger than one little President, and which crushed him with a gigantic vindictive metal fist." Matt brings his hand down on the table for emphasis, rippling the wine in the glasses sitting on every part of the table.

Truelove is making my friend upset. I wondered if I should ask about the Dutch bicycles now, ha-ha. But it was obviously the wrong time.

"Now, what do you think about film as another dimension?" Matt asks.

"Film is the encasement of a time interval," Truelove answers. "It is its own little time machine. If we could travel through time it would probably be with film, don't you agree with me?"

"Hmm." This has stopped Matt cold.

Jack is sitting, his back against the booth, gulping down his wine while his glasses reflected Truelove in two distinct but distorted fish-eye blobs. In the blobby reflection, Truelove's hands are still putting together pieces of an invisible puzzle in front of him and their distorted movement makes his hands larger, then smaller, in Jack's thick glasses.

"Matt," Truelove says, "I don't mean to make you upset, but sometimes getting upset with yourself is necessary when you face the truth."

Outside the restaurant, we say goodbye to the filmmaker and the museum director, as Matt begins muttering to us as Truelove walks down the wet street.

"He's an asshole. He's a fucking asshole," Matt says.

"Hey, shhhh. Don't say that." Jack holds him back.

"Let's go," Jack says.

MOVEMENT

To cross the U.S. quickly, I'd hop on a freight train box-car leaving Seattle and ride for two days to Chicago—then take an 8:00 P.M. hotshot to Albany. I could then hook up with the 6:40 A.M. out of Albany and that would land me in New Haven. So from there I'd hitch a local milk train into New York City.

Or I would sometimes ride on top of a car carrier tuning in the dashboard radio to a country-and-western station while stretching across a Lincoln Continental's front seat. I could look through the front windshield, across a pan-flat Kansas landscape, watching in almost complete silence but for a gentle-pedal steel guitar as we entered New Mexico and a Santa Fe station.

If I looked out for yard bulls, I'd be in L.A.'s Ana-heim yard as soon as I could say Disneyland.

If L.A. was where I wanted to be.

Sue said that Time exists in order to keep everything from happening at the same time . . . uh, in our universe.

"In other universes, time," according to Sue, "happens at the same time."

After talking with Sue over the phone, time and movement is something that I become very excited about.

When I was younger I had perfected the cross-country road trip, for instance. By road or rail. The trips were perfect. Stepping from one hotshot boxcar to the other, traversing the blurred roadbed below, my feet didn't even touch the ground as I changed freight trains while traveling. All the transients looked on incredulously with their road-dirty bearded faces.

I begin to move with easy, unstrained body movements in an effort to start marching around the house again. I haven't marched a lot lately but I needed to feel less like a cat sleeping in a store window.

One inch of movement or a cross-country trip could both be difficult, and could both be divine.

Movement provides life's questions and life's answers simultaneously.

I make informmercials that move. I attempt to move people with them. I try to move a product. I try to move the viewing cable television public off their butts, into their cars, down to the nearest Wal-Mart to buy a product that might cost them fifteen times what the product cost to make.

I have wanted to become a moving man as a professional follow-up to industrial-film making, imagining that it would be fun to move furniture, and pick up things around the house and move them from room to room, to practice moving in anticipation of the eventual career change.

I want to be big and strong. I am small, round and weak. I would make a bad moving man. The furniture in my house doesn't fit next to my body, I have to hold it way out in front of me because of my swelling stomach.

· · ·

Jack, he is quite a story. He is light. Where is he? I hope I will find him again. And Matt, what happened to Matt? Where the fuck do they go? They are so taken with disappearing. I must talk with them. I have to talk with them about their ideas. What do they think about? What the hell do they think about? I don't know. They are impossible to figure. I will never know. Perhaps they do not think at all. I need to find out more about Cowboy Nemo. I want to see the film too, this is so strange that a film exists when they have been talking about it as a screenplay. And TEEN.

This inspires me. I begin to review screenplay notes I have collected in a red-covered spiral notebook. Notes written down during the Saturday-long seminar on screenplay writing I took with Joanna and Steve.

One note reads: "The key to a character's performance in a movie is his or her movement from one state of mind to another. The characters in a movie move someplace, they do not stay the same. The story is also moving someplace, or it moves the characters someplace, it will not stay the same."

I am remembering the man whose lecture I recorded in those notes; his name was Dr. Driver. The doctor had a cap on backwards, which looked funny because he was over fifty as I am. He promised if you signed up to his one-day-long screenplay structure seminar you'd know as much, if not more about screenplay writing than the top Hollywood writers. The sign-up cost for each person in the class of thirty-five was $700.[36]

"Even if the movie story tries as hard as it can to not induce movement or not cause the actors to move," the note went on, "the audience will change as they watch the movie, and so the story and the action will change and move even when it doesn't physically change."

The seminar was held on an overcast day, which most people were very happy about because it would have been a disappointment to have to stay inside all day on a sunny Saturday. Dr. Driver was very short, as I remember, and gestured a lot by waving a rolled-up script in his hand. Sometimes he would use the script as a pointer to indicate things that he would write on the blackboard. Dr. Driver yelled out his statements so that everyone in the class could hear him.

"This is because time is changing," Dr. Driver said, "and since time is always changing, it forces the moviegoing experience to have movement, whether the movie is providing it directly or not.[37] A silent, blank (black?) screen played to an audience will form three distinct acts because the audience will naturally feel three acts on their own, when they sit in the dark.

[36] That's 35 times 700, which is $24,500. Not bad for a Saturday.

[37] This is the assumption behind early Warhol films. He would point the camera in one direction, sometimes framing something simple that didn't move, like, say, the Empire State Building, and then just run the camera. Time would take care of the rest.

"Actors will focus a great deal on this phenomenon. The actors' concern over the movement of their characters and how the characters change during a story is an honest and important concern. They are not merely trying to drive the director out of his mind . . ."

The seminarians laughed.

"No, they aren't . . ." Dr. Driver said, as the laughter, which sounded like the bleating of sheep, died down quickly because the attendees were feeling every moment slipping by in the $700 lecture.

The doctor turned around from the blackboard, where he had made three or four arched lines that were meant to suggest story and character movement fitting together, and he shook his head, looking at the floor.

". . . None of you are going to make it." He said this in a reserved tone that left a queasy feeling in the room, as if something walked into the room that nobody wanted to see. "Unless you work your ass off!"

I close the spiral notebook and I return to my screenplay, $-GREAT SKULL ZERO-$.

Taking the advice from some of my seminar notes, I realize that one of the important functions of this screenplay is to attempt to create story movement that an actor's character movement can play into. It must keep moving.

$-GREAT SKULL ZERO-$ is a simple fantasy action adventure about a group of futuristic pirates looking for the hidden treasure on a war-torn jungle island on a small planet orbiting Jupiter. The story labors over the planning, the getaway and the fighting over the buried treasure. The lead character's objective in the adventure, to actually hold the money in his hands, is deceptively the most uninteresting part of the story for the audience. The hidden treasure is the reward the space pirate gets after he has done a good job defending his treasure map by killing and slashing, and he gets the treasure at the end of the story.

I want to watch as long as the space pirate has a plan, but I don't want to see his plan stop by letting him find the treasure.

After the pirate gets to hold the money in his hands, and he is rich, what's he going to do then? I want to see something happen next, so the most logical direction to go in at this point is to have the money taken away from the space pirate. He loses the money. Yolandé Negrita steals the money away from Roentgen. This helps put the story in a nice family-oriented package, perhaps something that Disney might take a look at.

I don't want to watch the space pirate spending his money; for instance, sitting with a wench in his lap lighting cigars and Nubian slaves fanning him. A one-shot payoff. I would rather see the money sunk to the bottom of the ocean or shot into space so that it can keep moving. I want to see how his plan works until he is able to get the money, and then I want to see how it doesn't work, something to keep the money moving and the character moving.

The space pirate could spend the money on a surgical operation on his face to hide his identity and this would further the chase, and contribute to movement.

The informmercial is similar in that it doesn't concern the audience directly with the product. It concerns itself, like the movie, with movement and character instead of the immediate object of their concern.

A typical informmercial will play something like this: The teenaged host, Felix, sits on a barstool against a gray backdrop. The lighting is low, so that you only see a silhouette of him.

A smattering of recorded music introduces the commercial piece, smooth voices singing in unison, doo-doo-doo-doowaaaaa, a soft jazzy Ray Charles singers sort of appropriation, and in two seconds the music ends, the lights come up, the audience applauds, and loudly.

The lights are very bright. Everything has got to shine so that you are literally burning your message into the viewer's retinas. And we can see now, oh, there are kitchen appliances in the background we didn't notice before. And there is a wooden chopping block right over Felix's left shoulder. If your audience is paying attention, this is a grabber right there, yes, the old kitchen set. Hardly ever fails.

Felix waves both his hands at an overjoyed audience, and you would think by this reception that he has just come back a hero unscratched from a war.[38]

---

[38] There is a reason for this. Most informmercial programmers fought in one of our wars, and the viewers did too, so the most striking mood a director can set in the beginning of an informmercial is this "When Johnny Comes Marching Home Again" mood/thing.

We don't want to lose them in the beginning of the spot, so that's why there is so much joy in the beginning like there is. We want our viewers to be thinking: This is . . . uh . . . what the hell is this? So they don't go changing the channel on you.

Over the first hurdle we go, and Felix was absolutely the best at it. For a guy with no smile, he could turn the charm up full blast.

All right, now, Felix is going to signal to the audience to quiet down, because he is making it seem like he doesn't have much time. This is a very important maneuver, because you want the viewer to feel like the host of the show isn't going to waste his time, so he has to look like he doesn't have much time either, which is incorrect, because we have an entire thirty minutes, sometimes, my God, an hour, to fill with practically nothing.

This "time" maneuver also is signaling to our home viewers that this is going to be fast, and they are going to get what they are looking for (they don't actually know what that is yet) soon, so they don't have to worry about the channel changer, they are going to give this kid a chance. This brings to mind one of the reasons that so many of our informmercial presenters are teens. It's to play on the sympathy of the older home viewers who hopefully are just beginning to think: Well, that's a nice boy, he could be ours.

You might be thinking that this is too much, but there are no FCC restrictions on the pulling of heartstrings, yet.

Felix on the television stage

The director of the informmercial has to focus at all times, remembering each viewer out there is holding a little remote control in their hands,[39] so he is treading on

[39] When the remote control was invented, it made it so much easier for home viewers to change the channel and leave the commercial spot in the electronic dust that the commercial maker had to work three, no four times as hard as he did before that little invention. This was particularly true of the main target audience, who is over sixty, because in the old pre-remote days there was no way they were going to get up out of their chairs to change that channel, they'd just as soon let the program play all the way through the half hour just to see what might be programmed next. So the early pioneer informmercial makers had it easy, big time.

extremely thin ice right now. In a few minutes that pressure is going to go away because we are going to hook those suckers, I mean, viewers. Sorry.

"Okay then!" Felix says to his studio audience. "Sister Mary Reily called in to say that back at her house they are experiencing the cold weather that is sweeping up into the northern states today. Oooooohhhh." Felix shivers, wrapping both arms around his body.

"That just feels cold thinking about it, doesn't it? I'm glad that we are in this nice warm studio, aren't you?" Felix stands up from his chair after he says this.

Now this is practically a cookie-cutter opening; that is to say, it is one that has opened a lot of shows before, but it can really work. We have our reference to a religious belief, which is not completely committing to a parochial ideology. We don't have the Sister on the show, we just quickly mention her name, and that will go to work for us. You have your weather rundown, and that is going to cozy up most of your viewers. Make them feel like they too are in the warm studio under those blaring lights.

From this point Felix dovetails the show properly, introducing another guest, a woman who is about three years older than he is, named Sarah. Sarah begins to make a new cookie with a secret recipe all her own that she is going to give out, over the air, at the end of the show. The product is there, hidden on the set, until it is time to pull it out. We keep it hidden until the last minute. Until the guests have a problem.

There is difficulty with the cookie baking. Felix and his guest are growing concerned with a problem, but the audience is concerned with the guests.

"I should have cleaned my oven a little before the show, but I have been having problems with the cleaner I'm using," Sarah says. "It leaves a kind of, I don't know, smell."

The host and the guest become more and more interested in "finding" a product that will solve this problem that seemed to come out of nowhere, like most problems do.

"How many of you just can't get rid of that oven smell?" Felix prompts.

The audience gasps.

Of course the sexual connotations are almost but not quite obvious.

Cut to the audience, and every woman there is shaking her head no. The men are consoling the women. Some of them look like they are tilting their heads with concern, as if they are saying, "Well, honey, I didn't know that was a problem, we could fix that, couldn't we?"

I try to be careful and time it so at the precise moment that the product is needed, whammo, the presenter and the guests discover it behind the counter or desk or what-have-you. It is a surprise, and we didn't even know that there was a product. It was sitting behind the counter all the time. This is to keep things moving along, so they don't have to go and buy it, or whatever.

To further the movement, the product amazes the guests as it is put to use cleaning, scrubbing, wiggling and doing whatever it is that it does best. Then a price is mentioned, also a phone number. And through television osmosis, at the end of the half hour the viewers will want to buy it, and they don't even know why.

An informmercial is very similar to a pirate's stolen treasure in theme. Only the audience is the treasure.

"Another example of movement can be seen in the Monster Movie," the Saturday seminar instructor, Dr. Driver, was saying.

"The story concerns itself obsessively and to some, idiotically, with the chase and the dodge; running away and being pursued.

"At the moment when the monster catches the innocent young college coed, there is less action. The details of what the monster does with the young girl are of varying importance. It is what we *think* is going to happen to her. By actually showing it, the audience's own idea or fantasy of what might happen to a young college coed when she is caught by a monster might be disturbed," he said, having a young girl in the seminar group stand up and allow him to hold on to her tightly.

Dr. Driver was pantomiming the eating of the flesh of the captured young coed, by playing the part of the monster. Then he stopped to address the students.

"The audience might react by thinking: Well, that's

not what *I* would do with a young coed (if I were a monster)," he says as he pulls off a sort of Jerry Lewis double take with his rapt audience of paying students.

The seminarians laughed again, but cut this short, because it was the last hour of the all-day seminar.

"The Romance story is another example. The Romance is a dance around the idea of a relationship (SEX). But the sex itself is missing from the story. We see the characters before and after sex. We see them pursuing sex and we see the funny repercussions after they have sex, but the sex scene itself is a possible turnoff.

" 'That is not what I would do with a young coed if I were in bed with her.' " Dr. Driver tried his Jerry Lewis double take again but it bombed and nobody laughed.

"It is dangerous territory at least. Sex is not what the movie is about, although it is what drives the characters in the movie. This is because the sex itself does not move. Sex stops the story. It becomes subjective. Or it is harder to make it move for the viewer because he or she is not included in it."

Then he wrapped up the seminar, returning to the blackboard, where he has scribbled the names of different film genres.

Touching the board with a squeaky piece of chalk, Dr. Driver underlined the word "monster."

"The monster devouring

The Monster

the young girl does not move," the doctor said, "and the bank robber spending his money does not move. There are ways to put movement into these events, like what Alfred Hitchcock did in the shower/death scene in *Psycho*. He cut to a new shot every half second so the audience wouldn't get tired of the knife going up and down."

Suddenly this movie advice seemed somewhat restricted and preachy, as if I already knew what he was talking about. What was he talking about anyway, as if movies are made only a certain way? Hey, I had spent seven hundred bucks to come to this.

The thought seemed to be passing through the entire group of students. They were realizing that it was the end of the lecture and they didn't feel any smarter. They weren't.

"They weren't," I catch myself saying out loud, alone in my writing attic, and looking at these old notes. We were bamboozled. It was as bad as an informmercial. "Why didn't I know that?" I say aloud again, this time directing my speech at the kitty cat that is sitting on my desk.

The kitty blinks at me.

I resume writing my science fiction adventure screenplay . . .

The blind albino negroid centaurs live in a hilltop village surrounded by a vast savanna of cool lavender flame. In the center of the village is a Black Parthenon made of tires that houses their blind albino hermaphrodite negroid centaur oracle-chief attended by tiny eohippus-sized centaur siren-women who sing and cluster about the oracle singing from the scrolls that are recorded from the nightly somniloquys of the oracle by the bloodless braille-scribe putti who hang like green bats snoring and chuckling to themselves. The blind albino hermaphrodite negroid centaur has two penises and two vaginas. Its first set of genitalia is dainty and ornamental at the base of the humanoid torso, but is still fully functional and is often attended to by the eohippus-sirens who lick and copulate with the oracle, thus conducting the oracular charge into their bodies which causes them to be considered peripheral manifestations of the oracle so long as they are conjoined in the sexual act, and any shriek phrase or utterance is considered to be of the oracle himself and is fastidiously recorded by the ever-present scribes. The other set of genitalia is the horse penis and vagina, which are both robust in size and used to father and give birth to some of the finest mutant stallions in all creation: a two-headed green hermaphrodite Pegasus with dual mane of luminous flickering quills, a double-torsoed female centaur with a female torso at both ends of a modified horse body, an aquatic Medusa centaur that wraps its prey like a spider in glowing cocoons using threads it pulls from its spinnerette nipples.

Our saints are tie-dyed in legion with gold page and contro-verse-saying analogues to the human condition antelope maps, and absorbing speed we fade in the resonance of disappearance, a freshly birthed catalogue of invisibility made more miraculous by sound. A marriage of movement to a sound of defiance. Metapegasian cloud-gods reveal the lucid detachment and move silently onward . . .

I take a break from my screenplay wondering to myself if it is going to sell or not, turn off the typewriter, pull out the piece of pink paper (I've run out of white) twisted in the typewriter carriage, place the paper face down on a flimsy card table decorated at the corners with green and red birds. The card table is so flimsy it hardly holds the heavy typewriter. I think I need more action in my action screenplay so I write a note, ACTION, across the pink paper.

I decide to go downstairs, to search for a lost negative in my files. I am slowly starting to value the time I spend moving to simple destinations in my doddering old age. I'm beginning to believe that movement like this little trip downstairs, the movement itself, is what life is all about.

Bending under the sink to grab on to something unexplainable. Starting to gather up some papers left under there.

"Sweep your house, sweep your mind," the Zen Master said to the student.

Bumping my head on a sill or overhang.

Moving provides meaning for our humble (if still vicious) life of four-dimensional existence. Four-dimensional existence makes the frightening fox hunt into an entertainment, or war into a pastime or a sport. Even when evil is dull and monotonous, there tends to be a lot of movement, action and entertainment involved.

Maybe movies are evil.

As long as I am conscious of my dimensional being and the space around me, I am very happy just moving within the dimensions.

Even thought has fairly basic rules of movement, destination and accomplishment and it also has simple rewards.

Hey, Brutha,

Everything here is gettin' kinda rough. Some of tha townspeople in the place is lookin' for us because they want their money back for the Pink$_2$ rapture shit that we were tryin' to pull off for you on da side. We'll fix that up for ya, doncha worry about that.

I think that you might find dis kinda funny, though, the queer is onto us, because we fucked up with the movie you helped us make, sorry. But the fat guy named Harris we showed it to loved it, I think you are gonna be a fuckin' star. Funny shit, huh?

Do you know what a star is?

Anyway, the infomercial guy found out about the film. We fucked up but luckily he hasn't asked about the film lately. How in the hell can I keep all this little stuff in order, dates and such, I'm needin' a secretary. I know that is what

Matt is supposed to be doing, but he's drunk all the time. I'm not complainin'.

Yet.

Just kiddin' ya, Bro'.

peace, Jack

♠

Pink

THE INFOVENTION

Brandon and Bates Steel Saws is hosting an informmercial convention, or infovention, at a remote ski resort and
I want to be there. I had met with Matt earlier in the day,
and asked if he wanted to go to the convention and perhaps go skiing on the side. He sounded enthusiastic.

"Are you going to take me skiing, Spunky?" he said
as he rounded a pool table at a local bar. Matt loves
hanging out in bars, he sits in them and writes his poetry[40] and drinks, two of his favorite things. He can play
pool well too.

We leave from Matt and Jack's house, it's my first
trip to a remote ski resort. The furniture in their house is
scattered about the room haphazardly and some of their
Salvation Army chairs have the legs broken or cut off of
them, so when you sit down, you are nearly sitting on the
floor.

---

[40] Matt writes volumes of scratchy, beer-stained barroom poetry.
Spunky hasn't ever read any of it because he has never thought
to ask. Spunky doesn't particularly like poetry, but some of
Matt's poems go like this: "You sit there with your wife, And tell
me will you tell me, Curly rose of Tibet sitting like a wilted petal
on the end of a long tune, Pillow style life. (growl)" The growl
needs to be done with as much animal pain as the reader of the
poem can muster, which for Matt is a lot. When he reads this
poem in the late night hours of the bar, it scares the shit out of
the female bartenders and challenges the male ones.

Matt is looking good in a sort of pirate's getup. He had lost his front tooth recently when he was backpacking with a friend in Big Sur, so he is playing up a new pirate look. He is wearing a striped stocking cap, bell-bottoms that are loosely gathered about the waist with a big thick belt with a large buckle, a shirt that billows in an Errol Flynn sort of sea-pirate swashbuckler way and worn brown pirate boots. Matt grabs his bag, we say goodbye to Jack and we walk out the door on our way to the infovention. He says that he has to make a stop at the liquor store down the street before we catch the plane.

Matt buys one tall bottle of Ancient Age whiskey and a shorter bottle of Jack Daniel's whiskey in case he runs out.

I am greatly anticipating the infovention. Some outstanding informmercial producers and directors will be in attendance. I explain the event to a somewhat perplexed Matt. I tell him how they will have screenings at the small theaters in this little mining town, in Leadville, Colorado, and how everyone gathers in this one elegant little restaurant and shmoozes and talks about their projects. It is sometimes a lot of work, but also it can be fun.

I try to explain to him what it will be like when we get to the infovention, as Matt's head tilts like a dog trying to guess which hand the bone is in.

"It sounds awesome, Spunky," Matt says. "I mean, all those people. Oooo . . ." He shudders as if his whole body has turned to jelly and pours a shot of whiskey into the Coke he has ordered from the stewardess, who is in a bad mood.

"I'm just going to have to cheer her up today. Look how grumpy she looks, huh? We cannot have that, no sir," Matt chirps.

"How's it going today"—reading her name tag—"Sharon? How are you? Gonna be a nice flight, no?" Matt says as he watches her get a pillow down from an overhead bin, hand it to him and walk farther down the aisle.

"Hey, that was nice, I didn't even ask for a pillow," he says with amusement. Matt pours some more whiskey into his now half-finished plastic cup, narrowing his eyes on her figure. "She's gonna be all right."

Matt turns his head to the paper I have just tried to unfold in the limited seating space.

"Hey, what's that?" he asks, pointing to a weird photo of a goat.

In the front section of *The New York Times,* there is a story about a vampire loose in Puerto Rico.

"Hey, it's a story about a vampire. In *The New York Times,* yet," Matt says. "Is it real?"

"It has to be, it's in the *Times,*" I say as I check the section to see if it is a special joke insert or advertisement.

Nope, it's page four.

"It's a vampire story all right," I say. Our eyes bug out in a strange kind of amused fear, and we begin to read.

"It is a monster, look, it says that." Matt begins to paraphrase from the open article. "It is a monster!" and then he stops the waitress as she tries to get by us. "Could I have another Coke?"

"It is gray, has red eyes, a tongue that goes in and out of its mouth, and his back changes colors," Matt quotes from a man who apparently had seen the vampire. "A tongue that goes in and out of its mouth, I like that."

"We have to go there," I say.

"And forget about the infovention?"

"This is too good to be true," I say, ignoring Matt's last sentence. "Do you think that there are vampire hunters there?"

"Oh, yeah, of course," Matt says. "If it is such common knowledge, the vampire hunters must have come from all over the world to get in on this. This sort of thing doesn't happen every day. This is big. Puerto Rico has got to be crawling with vampire hunters."

"And media," I add with a rise of my eyebrows. "That too."

"Good combo," Matt says. "I mean, Coke and whiskey. It makes a good combo. You don't want any?"

"No, thanks. People are keeping their pets indoors because they are afraid the monster will bite them."

"Uh-huh."

Matt grabs his drink with both hands as the little plane begins to climb over the Rocky Mountains on our way to the infovention.

"I hate flying," Matt says.

"Why, because of the turbulence?"

"No, I like that part. I just get bored in this confined metal cylinder. Excuse me, ma'am. One more Coke?"

Matt smiles at the in-flight hostess. "She is not having a good day today at all."

"How can you tell that?" I ask.

"Oh, did you see the look on her face? Ooooo . . ." and he shivers again as if a little Gila monster is running up and down his spine.

I go back to the article about the other monster after I catch a glimpse of the worried look on the hostess's face.

"Hey, you're right, she is having a bummer. I wouldn't have noticed right off," I say.

"She is having a total bummer," Matt says.

"We could ask Sabene for some money to go to Puerto Rico and look for the monster," I say. "Sabene owns the saber company that I have made informmercials for."

"Oh, that would be . . . yeah, I mean, yeah! That would be so . . ." and Matt squints his eyes, pointing in front of his nose as if he is typing on the tiny little typewriter in front of him. Again making the gesture that he makes when he thinks something is right on. He makes this tiny typewriter gesture whenever he hears a particular song he likes on a tape that he has brought with him and plays over and over again.

"That would be so . . . awesome," he finally says.

"We could pose as vampire hunters, you and I, with special hunting suits rigged out with clips and ropes and spears and knives and things."

"Yeah, there could be a special insignia on the arm."

"We could pretend that we actually caught the monster, and issue a press release saying that we are going to unveil the monster at the San Juan Holiday Inn, and we could prepare a convention room, and have the monster inside of a cage, with curtains in front of it, that part on command, just when we are confident that the attendees are in the right mood."

"And the monster could spit blood on the curtains, which would be white, and make a horrible noise, just before we pulled the curtains back."

"And it would be a guy in a suit," I say.

"Dressed as the monster."

"A hoax."

"Would we get away with that?" Matt asks.

"For a little while, but then we might have to make a run for it."

"And we would have it all on film because we would be filming it," Matt says. "It would be so . . . cool," and then again he makes that gesture of the tiny typewriter.

And I just stare at him doing that, making that gesture.

"I think that we should still go to the infovention," I say.

"Oh, yeah, I guess we should. But later, after we do that, we could go to Puerto Rico."

"Hmm." I am thinking that we could do it. We might be able to get some money to do it.

Matt looks at me and believes me. How cute.

He says, "Take ahold of this moment, Spunky, ride it, don't let it get away from you without acting on it." And then as if he were delivering a line in an old 1930s high-seas costume adventure, he says, "We have to go to Puerto Rico to find the vampire!"

The plane is just then touching down, the rubber wheels that were the size of my car kiss the runway once, then twice, then finally we are on the ground.

Matt shivers again. I am beginning to think that this is a result of serious alcohol problems, DTs perhaps rather than what I originally thought, that they were shivers of appreciation, or inspiration. Hmm.

We pick up our rented Chevy Blazer and head west out of Denver to the ski resort where they are holding the infovention.

"The atmosphere is a far cry from Las Vegas, I'm gonna tell you that right now," I say to Matt, "which is why they have this thing up here in the mountains away from the desert. Change of atmosphere. You are going to see a lot of fur coats and cellular phones walking up and down the small mining town street, Matt. I hope that doesn't turn you off."

"It probably will," and he takes a sip of his stashed whiskey.

We are late to the infovention. We pull into town and leave our bags in the car to look for the Braying Donkey Restaurant, where my friend Heidi is holding a little get-together with her promotional team that is pushing their informmercial item, Robin Shoes. Robins are shoes that you can walk around in but you can also use them for advanced rock climbing outings, a sort of two-in-one shoe.

After everyone has tired of watching each other's informmercials, and have finished viewing the new equipment on display in a huge ski lodge at one end of town, all they have left to do is party and shmooze.

"Hey, Spunky!" a voice cries from Heidi's table as we are approaching. I realize the person sitting at the table is an old friend, Stewie, whom I haven't spoken to since he sued me over a botched informmercial deal we had attempted to put together somewhere in the distant past.

Man-oh-man, why does he have to be here, crowding my holiday? Of course the only seat left at the table is right next to Stewie, so I try to be social and sit down next to him, introducing Matt to the others.

"OH, THIS IS GREAT!" screams Stewie, in an overly loud and overly excited voice. There seems to be a great deal of leftover est love-vibe remaining in Stewie's cheery demeanor. A forced effervescent giddiness, which has possessed him ever since we met in '88. I used to like it, but now I realize that it can be deadly. All that love can turn into intense bursts of target-sharp hate, and I have had the displeasure of being that target.

"Hey, Stewie, I didn't know that you'd be around," I say.

"I WOULDN'T MISS THIS! NO! I COME EVERY YEAR!" He screams, which reminds me that everything that Stewie ever says is an exclamation. He never has any other structure to his statements. He'll say "GREAT!" not just "Great."

"HOW HAVE YOU BEEN! WE HAVEN'T SEEN EACH OTHER SINCE I DON'T KNOW HOW LONG!" Stewie says.

"Okay, I guess, you know, you have got to take the bad with the good."

"I KNOW!!"

"It figures you'd know," I say in a challenging tone, but Stewie does not take the challenge.

"I DO KNOW!!"

Standoff.

Why did he sue me?

Out the corner of my eye, I realize that Matt has strayed from the table and is now standing next to the singer onstage, sort of hippie-grooving, rolling his loose fists in small circles next to his shoulders. And seesawing his head back and forth like his chin was perpetually swinging a weight tied to the end of it. I look over to check the place at the table next to Heidi. There are four empty drink glasses sitting on the table that Matt has left behind. Heidi smiles at me and looks back at Matt.

The lead singer clearly wants Matt to leave the small stage but Matt persists, and loses himself in his dance. I flash on the disruption at the Umpire Awards in Sasquatch.

A sort of cold fear comes over me.

The food is served late, and Stewie and I talk for an eternity, as we used to when we were friends. Other informmercial presenters and producers are circulating from table to table, hugging each other, shmoozing, chatting, making deals to make more informmercials. There is more bad breath here than anywhere in the world, I think to myself.

Occasionally someone comments that they are sorry that Felix Arroyo died.

"An unfortunate incident," they say. Then they always ask me, "How was he to work with?"

I always find that odd.

Now the lead singer on the stage, in an attempt to get Matt away from him, is walking back and forth singing a Van Morrison song as if Matt weren't standing right next to him, and spastically pushing him with his body by just running into him. Matt easily gets pushed because he is in his dancing reverie, and he is feeling the whiskey now. How much has he had? But luckily he gets right back up there and stands next to the singer as if he hasn't been pushed out of the way.

"LOOK AT MATT!!!" Stewie screams.

To Stewie's delight, Matt gets pushed over by the lead singer again and again, but I start feeling nervous, as though something horrible is going to happen to Matt.

By the time something really horrible does happen to Matt (the singer grabs him and throws a punch which doesn't land on Matt but on the ride cymbal next to Matt's head), we have to leave because there is another party that everyone is going to.

I am particularly shmoozy with my Saber client, for whom I have made more than sixteen informmercials over the last few years. His name is Kenny Sabene[41] and

[41] Kenny Sabene is a megastar in the informmercial world. He is a networker and very devoted to his friends. He keeps his acquaintances informed of his comings and goings to and from their

he has created a huge mail-order CD market worldwide and also was close friends with Felix Arroyo and had played music with Felix's band more than once.

Sabene helped Felix and his band decide instrument endorsements. Sabene and other friends of Felix's form a curious bond. I am one of them, huddling against the cold and heartless world after Felix has died. But we vigilantly keep his memory alive.

We should develop a secret handshake.

All the friends and business acquaintances who have been keeping in touch with each other by cellular phone are going to the Dome, which is an inflatable arena they are using to put on a rock and roll concert featuring Jim Bock and the '70s band Diva. So Matt and I go to the Dome.

There are fresh tire tracks in the snow leading up to the Dome. Thousands of people are walking in and out of the place. This coaxes the words "what a spectacle" from my lips as I pull over to the side of the road in our rented Chevy Blazer. Matt has Speechless blaring from the Blazer's stereo and is pointing partly at the speaker where the sound is coming from and also just down a bit

---

local neighborhoods and countries because he is traveling so much. He is very short and in his late fifties. He is a great talker and is balding, so he has a hair weave.

toward the ground as if he is trying to point to the notes individually as they come out of the speaker and pass by his gesturing hand.

Stewie is in the back seat all but screaming in pleasure, "THIS IS GREAT!! OH, MATT, THIS IS GREAT!!" Matt has just about had it with Stewie at this point.

Matt is extremely sensitive about riding in the car with two fags like us. He is waiting for us to pull something. He is afraid to go to bed tonight because he probably thinks that I am going to sneak into it while he is asleep. But the Speechless music occupies him for the moment.

We find ourselves walking down a snow-covered road still on our way to the Dome, and Matt, inspired by his five-thousand-feet-above-sea-level drunk, is prancing toward the guitar sound and the lit-up concert dome but strays every now and then because he sees people that he has to talk with about the show and about how it sounds. Stewie herd-dogs Matt back onto the snow-covered road with a certain regularity, so Matt doesn't get lost. I venture ahead, trying to make it to the front door to meet Sabene.

Diva is playing when we get there. I stand transfixed, trying not to attract attention, because I don't want to dance. The whole place is slam dancing, it seems, because the young spokesmodel crowd is here, and they are having their fun.

Sabene appears like an apparition from the dance

floor. He is sweaty and has been dancing all night. As he talks with me, he is still on his cellular phone to Japan, talking business. He is wearing a brocade floor-length jacket and has cut almost all the hair off his head. His sideburns are shaved into spiral pattern.

"It's the new thing," Sabene says.

Heidi pulls my jacket and says that she was just backstage and Matt was being led out the exit door by a large security guard. But miraculously there he is, holding three drinks for us.

I begin to talk with Heidi and Sabene. As we chat, my eyes scan the dance floor. Wherever I look, Matt seems to be integrated into the scene.

Slam dancers at the front of the stage are raising Matt above their heads. He is still holding his drink.

I glance over Heidi's shoulder and see Matt being shown the door by security.

Looking to my right, there's Matt singing onstage next to Diva's lead guitarist.

Seconds later Matt walks up and introduces two young informmercial kids to me, one from Sasquatch and one from Russia.

He returns a split second later with more drinks for everyone, drinks that he has pilfered off the tops of round tables that are placed all around the dome.

Matt is moving awfully fast.

Matt is asking this Russian girl for her telephone number. She wants to dub Russian informmercials and sell the Russian products here in the States.

Matt can hardly speak, he just goes "Ooohhhh . . . !

Can you believe her!" behind her back when she isn't listening. Then he shivers as though he is cold, but it is hot in here.

"Go hang with her, Matt, invite her out, that's something that these infoventions are good for, meeting people," I say.

"I don't know what to say to girls like her. I always get so nervous." He sighs. "Russia!"

We leave in our Chevy Blazer without the girl, but Matt has her phone number. Stewie says, "THAT WAS GREAT!! WASN'T THAT GREAT, MATT?!! MATT?!!"

"Huh?" Matt says, only allowing himself the smallest interruption from his intense stare directly into the five-inch elliptical dash speaker, as if he can see Speechless playing inside the dash.

"WASN'T THAT GREAT?!!" Stewie screams.

"Yeah-yeah . . ." The distant expression and dim glow off the surface of his face makes it look like he is one of a million faces at an arena show. "Yeah."

I was going to tell him how beautiful that look was, but I was afraid that he would be offended, so I didn't say anything.

"I gotta find a guitar," Matt says as he looks up from the speaker.

🌲

When I return to Sasquatch, there are fresh tire tracks on the lawn outside my house. New black-and-brown tire tracks that have dug up the ground. A teenage excavation party; looking for kicks. I wonder if they found any.

The teenagers must think it's funny. I feel old. I feel helpless. I feel singled out. Why me? They must feel the same way.

I work a little bit more on my science fiction action adventure screenplay that I hope to sell someday, $-GREAT SKULL ZERO-$.

Yolandé Negrita lounges in a green basalt bath-tub, a rhino-beetle with a tiny candle on its back crawling up her arm. The entire floor of the room is covered in rhino-beetles with candles on their backs crawling about along with thousands of other beetles of the Umbonious Crassicornus species. In each corner of the room stand small shrines with fetishes and different forms of incense burning. One is a large golden Nautilus shell with tentacles of Frankincense, surrounded by sea-fans lit from behind revealing the antics of tiny sprite-boys playing leapfrog and biting at each other's nipples. Another is an Iron Bulldog with smoke pouring from its nostrils surrounded by a bonsai forest of pines where hang tiny chimes. In one corner there is a large black stone snake sur-rounded with flower petals and purple wasps flying in and out from the center of the coil. And last there is a giant Roman coin as big as a man spinning perpetually in the corner, and pictures of twisted ladders flash on the walls from holes in the floor. Hanging from the ceiling are different types of bladders with different liquids in them. Many birds are there in the room: Quetzals, Ibis, Baby Roc, two-headed birds with human feet, birds with snake heads, winged snakes, and crimson bats. Yolandé Negrita is singing. She pulls on a long red ponytail hanging from the ceiling and a sparkling rope ladder falls from a porthole that slides from above her with a silvery hiss. Reaching this upper deck, she proffers her nipple to the smallish Chinese woman whose ponytail hangs through the floor. The Chinese woman greedily licks and sucks at the nipple which is always painted with a strong hallucinogenic tincture falling into a reverie of ecstatic ululations calling to the spirit of Koxinga to make her children strong and brave. Yolandé Negrita takes the frog-shaped bottle from around her neck, unscrews the head/cap brush and proceeds to repaint her nipple with quick back-and-forth strokes.

Yolandé Negrita says, "Mind is tidal, its vastness oceanic. This is the shoreline of Techgnosis, endless beach, infinite coves. When we join it we become it."

Giant Sea Snail glides along the beachhead of Mind floating on iridescent ooze, ambergris-gris/ecto-lube, shell terminating into the sky, shell modulating into castle, paradise of the symbiotes read as Munsalvaesce read as utopian materialism in a world outside history. Monadic nomads of the leisure class, Gilell and

Isstari vibrate in unison and synchronize to the joy-hum of the beatitude host, all is convivial, a granphantasmaguignol of sparklingmad delicacies, theater in a time of postcultural mythopoesis, biopoesis.

Pink

I continue writing until my cat is asleep, the fire in my stove has gone out and the darkness has done a belly flop so the sky is morning-bright again.

I read an article about Paul Spottick, the Chairman of the Board of Dynosaur Communications (a cable network and informmercial production company). There is an accompanying picture that depicts Paul at his office desk, posed in a ritualistic and prestigious manner, king of communications, ruler of the roost, or what-have-you, and on his desk is a book, *How to Sell Good Product*. This may have a bit of tongue-in-cheek about it, the book may have been given to Paul by a friend as a joke. But selling a product isn't a joke. It's not even fun. You run into funny situations making and selling good products and some people think of filmmercials as a joke— but I laugh at those people. I laugh a hearty Douglas Fairbanks laugh before the closed gates of viewer buying conscience, amusing Sabene Sabers and their forty thieves. The gates sometimes remain closed. Unless you know the magic words to open them. That is what a filmmercial maker tries to tell an executive in the offices of Dynosaur—that he knows the magic words to open a floodgate of 1-800 calls, ensuring that millions of dollars will spill his way. And those magic words are reverently handed to the man in the Black Tower at Dynosaur, in the form of a informmercial product concept. Jack and Matt and I can write that concept, I know it.

Jack tells me he knows a lot about Las Vegas. Interesting. He lived there once, he says.

In Vegas, a filmmercial maker will inevitably find himself in the office of an executive like Paul, telling him the angle of his next informmercial.

"What kind of commercial are you making?"

"A commercial that will sell a lot of product," Product Sales being one of the many "standby" and boring magic terms in many a commercial front office.

"That sounds like a good idea." Money talks at Dynosaur.

If you get the job, then you find out you will have to deal with the System, which I don't like. Even though you begged for the job in Paul Spottick's office, once you get what you begged for, you feel you don't want it anymore. This is because of the way the informmercial System works.

For one thing, every given person in each part of the System is afraid of the other people in the other parts of the System. The executives frighten each other. They in turn frighten the writers and directors, and it is up to the producers to yell at them that they are frightening everyone. Why are they frightened? Is it their entanglement in the corporate web? Clusters of little hands all working the controls of the machine,[42] and attempting to make one decision at a time? They base their opinions on the opinions of others. There is Nu-speak.[43] They have their own axioms and one-liners to tell each other why things are the way that they are. One of which isn't "Too many cooks spoil the broth." America went corporate one hundred years ago, and the commercial houses now work for the corporations. Gone are the days when an autocrat would sit behind a desk wired to his own butt intuitively making decisions about his commercials.

There is a strong suspicion that none of the executives working under the banner of Filmmercialhaus (which is an association of like-minded capitalist filmmercial entrepreneurs) was trained in an area even remotely related to informmercials. None of the executive officers have any sensitivity for drama. They work their way through other corporate establishments, like food products for instance, or clothing, and if they fall as they are climbing their various corporate ladders, they find themselves running a commercial house instead of a food or insurance division.

They insist that all corporate numbers can be juggled alike, and that you can test anything to show how it is going to perform.

There is a problem. Insurance. Everyone is so depen-

---

[42] A sentence stolen from *Something* (he inadvertently is responsible for the death of his son) *Happened* by Joseph Heller.

[43] A term from *Stranger in a Strange Land,* a new lexicon.

dent on it in our middle-class structure that the insurance companies got big enough to buy every large corporation in sight; businesses are run by insurance companies. And insurance companies want me to have insurance.

"How can I insure that my filmmercial is going to make them X amount of dollars? This is frightening," I say to the six executives, four men, two women, sitting around a conference-room table.

"I can't. Can't."

"Is your boat insured?" one of them responds, with required reserve.

"What?"

"Well, if your teenage daughter and her drunk friends steal it one night," another one of the executives points out, "crashing into a billion-dollar yacht moored nearby, what would you do then? Hmm?"

"What about your house?" another of them chimes in. "Is it insured?"

Oh, and am I supposed to insure the next seat-of-the-pants crapshoot of a decision I make?

"You said it, we didn't." Five out of the six executives smile at me.

So what it comes down to is, I must explain to my particular group of executives (who develop a report which is reviewed quarterly by their executives) why an individual working for the corporation chooses to spend five hundred thousand dollars airing a particular film-mercial. If there are no test numbers to back up a promotional spending decision because the informmercial didn't test well at Inform,[44] the mistake is punishable by fire (or being fired). A filmmercial to them is nothing more than a Widget. I am required to show my group of executives a number. Numbers are inevitable. I have to contract an analysis number from a test audience, through the loathsome organization Inform, because the ultimate test number suggests to my group of executives how much to "inform" the viewers by airing this particular informmercial.

The audience analysis number, or AAN, can range anywhere from zero (which is pretty much impossible to get, and if a commercial ever scored a zero, I would like to see that commercial) to one hundred, which is the best. A normal AAN is seventy-five. Just like high school! And if your AAN is below acceptable, say fifty, then forget it, your project will go no further. Either the AAN in-

[44] Inform is a privately run business separate from the commercial production companies. A man named Jobene Burell came over from France and talked all the corporate heads into using his "double-blind" statistical testing technique for their sales performance research. Burell even sold the idea to commercial production houses, guaranteeing they could tell scientifically how a commercial was going to perform by sending it through his test, for a fee of course. The double-blind idea is set up so that not only are the test subjects unaware of what is going to be tested on them, but the guys running the test do not know what they have just tested when they review their subjects, which apparently gives them a very clean and unbiased "number." In the informmercial business this is called the audience analysis number.

dicates that people liked the informmercial or you retest for a new AAN. The AAN cannot, according to my six executives, under any circumstance be a number that indicates that people do not like the filmmercial.

If an individual like me ventures to make a media-buying decision based on individuality, one outside the umbrella of the analysis number, the individual will be "individualized," knocked out of the corporation, as fast as a metal shooting range duck is hit with a pellet gun.

So Inform holds the cards. And if I go out on a limb and convince my executive group to air an informmercial that doesn't get a high score, and the limb doesn't break, then I don't get the glory anyway. There is no reward system for going out on limbs. Of course not. It goes unnoticed. I may get a nod from a junior division vice president, who is so scared himself that he won't look up from his cup of coffee. In other words, it is all on paper, and verified. And "safe." Nobody makes a decision on a hunch, because there is no percentage in it. And it is very hard for the creative people, who only make decisions on wild hairy hunches, to understand and communicate to these six executives.

If we were all executives, we would understand. I try to understand. I try to be understanding. The informmercial business works this way and I'm guessing that the movie business must work in the same way since it is corporate as well.

.   .   .

I would like to think the ancient ancestor of the filmmercial maker is the cave painter etching running deer and star shapes into the side of a quiet, smoky, torchlit cave . . . but more likely the filmmercialist's ancestor is the storyteller. Storytellers have the same problem. They are up against tough audiences too. In prehistoric times, the storyteller who comes up with a bad story is stoned to death by his bored listener/hunters. (Like the present-day filmmercialist who is low-numbered to death by his bored studio audience.) Is the prehistoric storyteller stoned to death because he told the wrong story? Or he told the story wrong? Maybe he didn't cut to the product soon enough for his funky caveman audience, half listening while gorging themselves on rotting venison. They heard it better the week before; maybe from the same storyteller! So they kill him . . . why not?! Then they eat him.

This same thing will happen to the filmmercialist who "pitches" the wrong commercial concept to the funky modern executives gorging on fresh sushi in a candlelit situation blithely mirroring the ancient past. If the filmmercialist tells the story wrong or the wrong story, the executives figuratively kill him. Then they eat him.

The concept pitch is a mock story, to simulate what the commercial will feel like to a home audience. It is easier to pitch a product concept than it is to sell the product, because you can slip in things like, "Then the viewers will want to buy our product." Whereas when selling a product, you have to get them to pick up the phone and dial. If you can pitch the story without using crutches like this, then it will be infinitely better. Although your audience of executives may not notice how clever you are being.

Another difference is, the point of the pitch is to sell the commercial concept to the executives. The point of airing the commercial is to sell the product to the audience.

Pink

147

One resident of Sasquatch, Buzz Post, a "real filmmaker" who goes to H/wood to pitch his movie stories, told me that if he is pitching a story about "The Giraffe" and it isn't working, he starts telling them the story about "The Bear," and if that is putting the executives to sleep or in any way rubbing them the wrong way, then he switches gears and starts to tell them about "The Snake." (He actually said that.)

"So," Buzz says, "at an everyday Movie-Town watering hole, people are telling so many stories that are different animals, you forget whether you are in Hollywood or the jungle. Ha-ha"—that Buzz, he goes for the cornball joke when he can.

I am so jealous of him that I have to say that I don't care for him very much, but live and let live, I guess.

Buzz says a good movie to him would simply be a movie with a good story. "Your sound can suck. You can have bad acting. You can get away with bad continuity and bad photography. But your movie will be strong if it has a remarkable story. An audience will weather almost anything to get at a good story.

"This is the one rare Movie Business democracy," Buzz goes on, "because everyone has some good stories to tell. Think of the old guys who sit outside the Feed Mill and General Store who get all excited when once a year Clem, who never says a word, decides that he is going to tell a story. They're excited because when Clem tells a story it usually is a really good story.

"Let me tell you, Spunky, I have a friend who never stops telling stories. From the moment that she comes over to my house for a visit to the moment that she leaves, she is telling one story after another. She is in a permanent stream-of-consciousness storytelling furor, flipping from one subject to the next. Being cued by interruptions, she mixes anecdotes from her experiences; her parents' experiences; her immediate surroundings; things that she overhears, dreams and desires of past, present or future; factual or imagined. These stories are told for any purpose, and with or without much detail into a nonstop babble of pure narrative action. She's like a television set constantly changing channels, and most of what she says is good story material. Except for the fact she is not editing herself, she is a storytelling genius. If I tape-recorded her for just one visit I would have enough material to make two or three films.

"All this is to say that 'I don't know any good stories' is not any excuse for the young filmmaker. You may not recognize a good story, but they are all around you all day long and when you go to sleep, the stories continue offering themselves to you in your dreams."

Hmm . . .

"People like to listen to the same story told to them over and over again," Buzz says, on a roll, as per usual.

"If one keeps in mind that one is telling a story that has been heard a thousand times before, storytelling can be less of an obstacle for a filmmaker.

"I know that after I hear someone tell a good story there is often the familiar comment, in that high-pitched whiny voice, 'That would make a good movie.' The familiarity of events and the logic suggests something that we have heard before, the classic (programmed) story, but in a new package so as to suggest a 'good movie.' Bright, interesting, original, arresting, instructional, with snap, crackle and pop—already heard one thousand times before.

"You know how many times a child asks for the story that has been read so many times before that the cover has worn off the book and the parent has long since handed the job over to Grandmother? And if a new storybook is introduced, the child goes into fits of insane rage; he must have the *same story!* Adults are similar, but they like to think that the story they are hearing is different somehow than the one they heard before, but in the end all they want to hear is the same story. Good really means: familiar."

Buzz really is full of it sometimes.

Swifty really is odd. He bungee-jumps. He has a good butt, and he uses this to play with people. He is one of the foremost presenters that Las Vegas Young Star talent scouts have seen. People are complaining about his behavior. He just wants to leave. But he can't, he needs to be in front of a camera, he is addicted to it. He needs footage. He finds himself in the footage; but not really. He should, it would help. Maybe he will get better. Maybe he will find his dad after all. That is what does it, I think, he doesn't have a dad. And he needs one. When he thinks that you are paying attention to him he acts like you are his dad and you get hit hard with some outburst or attitude. Then he forgets that he did it. His dad probably forgot too. Odd.

He likes to bungee-jump, that is his favorite thing, and I guess that it always will be until the end of time. He bungee-jumps constantly in Las Vegas from the top of the Mirage.

He was somewhat friendly with Felix, who protected him. Felix understood him. But even Felix couldn't help him. Swifty told me a little story of the only time that he had sex with Felix.

It was during the Flamex Compound informmercial shoot that Felix sensitively took his shirt off in the back of his warm rented Winnebago. He stood in front of Swifty and slowly began to rub his chest and stomach. Swifty was lying down on the bed in the Winnebago holding a joint.

"God, I'm horny," Swifty had told me Felix said.

Swifty watched as Felix pulled down his pants, revealing that he was not wearing any underwear, his dick springing up out of his lowered pants and standing perpendicular to his body.

Felix looked down at his dick as Swifty could feel his own swelling in incremental beats that went along with his ever-faster-pumping heart . . .

And that's as much as he would tell me.

"Why won't you tell me the rest, Swifty?"

"Because, man, it's private. Okay?" he said.

I heard an awful story about Swifty's dad, who kept Doberman pinscher dogs in the house, that when his dad died of a drug overdose, the dogs, who were hungry, ate his head off of his body. Funny, I didn't think that there was a lot of meat in the head, unless they ate the brain.

No wonder Swifty bungee-jumps.

Felix protected Swifty. He protected him and took care of him.

Swifty jumping off the Mirage

I'm remembering Felix in Japan. We are together, walking up a misty hillside toward a Buddhist temple in Kyoto. Felix laughs because we have walked for miles, something that Felix hasn't counted on, he is wearing rope-soled slippers that are wearing out. There are young Japanese girls carrying origami faces of Felix. Offerings made by futuristic (?) beings from a more advanced design dimension.

Even though Felix was Las Vegas' most influential informmercial talent, there was no contract that would ever bring him back. There was no offer big enough to make destiny reconsider and turn the deal around. He was last seen lying on the main artery of cheese (the Strip) in the town that gave him his chance. The town that he hated, and needed so badly. He evaporated from all the heat. I feel a small knot developing in my throat as I remember my friend.

He was my ombudsman.

In the papers there are new stories about folks that have been ripped off by the Two. There are some disappointments, they were supposed to rapture. And now the Two are missing. Apparently they have taken all of the money that people gave them. The money that was a sort of guarantee that they would be accepted into the ascension. Fools. Some had even sold their property. Now they are looking for them, the Two.

That's too bad, because I wanted to meet the Two. But also it is lucky, because I would have given them all the money that I have, which isn't much. But now they are on the lam, my faith and my money are safe.

Πινκ αλτ. υνιϖερσ.

I get up in the mornings and I reflect on my past mistakes. I think about the shopping habit that I had developed before I went bankrupt. I remember that I knew every item in every warehouse, and how much everything was going for at any time during every season. I even obsessively followed markdown seasons, and separate sale items on men's and women's clothing, automobiles, food and vacation packages. But the big thrill was the log loaders and the trucks. It became a full-time occupation that took away from my more stable life as a rock star. My friends became concerned, but would only indulge me by asking my advice when they needed to shop. Cameras held a special fascination.

My downfall was when I started to collect too much unneeded heavy machinery. Just the storage was thousands a week. Before I stopped I had acquired, by various means, seventeen log loaders, five earthmovers, six cement trucks, a variety of farm tractors, bulldozers, threshers and combines. Three log transporters. And one very rare steam engine with passenger cars and caboose.

I have a cigarette in the back area of the Cloudy-Bright Rehab mansion. A few of the other inmates are there smoking away. Little white puffs hanging over the smokers in the heavy and humid morning air. The city is still asleep. The tops of the buildings all around the back courtyard are all you can see, there is no view. Just a bunch of terra-cotta. The other patients shy away from me or laugh when I tell them that I have a shopping disorder. When I stand up and say my name and that I am an alcoholic, cross-addicted bargain shopper, they ask me: Are you for real? It may not be real to them but it is very real to me.

Lonnie and I are hanging out in the cafeteria of the mansion. He is telling me this funny story about an apartment that he once rented. It became available after a guy named Shirtless moved out. His name was Shirtless, because he went without a shirt all the time and also had a very built-up body. Lonnie met Shirtless a few times when he took over the apartment. And Shirtless was real nice to him, because he let him have some of the leftover furniture in his apartment. Stuff that he didn't need. When Lonnie was completely moved in, he found one of the things that Shirtless left behind was a diary. Since he didn't really know Shirtless, Lonnie felt free reading the diary, it was fair game as far as he was concerned. He was surprised to find that the diary is very explicit, and the entries are packed with detail. In the diary, Shirtless had these desires that he writes about where he fancies a woman to dominate him. He dreams of finding a woman who can discipline him and boss him around. A few months go by where the entries in the diary have Shirtless frequenting a number of male S&M bars where the customers either watch or participate in discipline exercises, humiliations and other routines on small staged areas. Shirtless watches for a few weeks, and is interested but only as an observer. He writes in his diary of all the different kinds of dominative and submissive themes he witnesses. He eventually partakes in a spanking session which he likes somewhat but he realizes what he really desires is a strong woman to take charge, and that he aspires to eventually find someone that wants or needs someone like him to be with.

A few weeks after Lonnie read the diary, Shirtless called Lonnie and said that he left some things over there, and he wants to come and pick them up. Lonnie told Shirtless that there is a pile of stuff in the closet, and that he hasn't thrown anything away, so he can come over to get it if he wants to. When Shirtless arrived, he was with a large woman. While Shirtless got his stuff, including the diary, from the closet the large woman was eying two packing crates beside the sofa. She asked Shirtless about them and he said: I didn't need them, so I just left them here in case Lonnie needed them. She said: You mean you gave away two perfectly good crates? And she gave him a look as if saying: When I get you home, you are going to get the beating of your life. A worried but satisfied expression came over Shirtless' face. So Lonnie was able to see the continuation of the fantasy as written in the diary, played out in real life.

J ack calls! He still wants to talk, but I am busy writing. Writing about them! I never thought that I would be too busy for them, Jack and Matt. They are hitchhiking to a distant rock concert event tomorrow. I tell them to use my name at the gate and then maybe they can get in; fat chance, it sounded good when I said it. I tell them Heidi is giving away free shoes behind the stage, that maybe they could throw her name around. Jack is calling from Matt's apartment and Matt is playing guitar in the background (not that well). We hang up.

Then Jack calls back. He wants to know the name of the shoe girl again. I tell him Heidi, Matt knows her. He says that Matt's apartment has just been robbed. He says that they just went out to play basketball and when they came back all the furniture was turned upside down. But he only called a few minutes ago. Maybe it was a short game of basketball. Speed basketball, that's probably what they play nowadays. Kids are so alien to me now. I didn't even know Jack played basketball. Maybe that's why they didn't play very long. The guitar is still there, it wasn't stolen. They don't know what happened. Freaky. They may have knocked the furniture over when they left and were too stoned to remember when they returned. They are going to go out and see a movie about a cyborg (?), *Johnny Mnemonic,* and drink beer. We hang up.

157

Next day I'm having breakfast with Matt at the Rubber Neck. He tells me a story about his past, when he was in junior high school outside of Austin. It was hot in Austin, and Matt likes the heat, he wishes that it was hotter in Sasquatch.

He begins the story. It is about a gang. He says: There are four of us in our gang. John H., John D., Jim and I. We are coming home from Middlesex Junior High School every day and playing golf in the hot weather, which is what we, as gang members, do in our town in 1985. Matt is gesturing in a very specific way, cutting the air with his left hand.

Matt says, "Since we are together so much and have just seen the movie *West Side Story* on videotape, we decide to name ourselves. Singing, 'When you're a Jet, you're a Jet all the way, from your first cigarette, to your last dying day.' We try out a few names for our new gang to the tune. 'When you're a . . .' A . . . 'King.' An 'Ace.' What are we? We're wise guys, I know, but . . . We settle on the 'Coolies,' not only because of the exploited Chinese labor force that built America's railroad system but because we are, of course, cool. 'When you are cool, you are cool all the way . . .' We're the coolest kids that we know about in our neighborhood. And we know that to be truly cool is to assume the derogatory nickname and the manner of an outdated, subservient, humble but aware Asian-American sect that practice Buddhism as well as smoke opium but do not spit on the railroad tracks of their overlords even though they should.

"We do things late at night like sneak out of the house and ring neighborhood doorbells to annoy people, or we drink stolen whiskey from our parents' liquor cabinets. We are eleven years old. We choose gang nicknames we fashion after playing cards. I am the Ace of Clubs, and the others are Aces of Diamonds, Spades and Hearts. The four Aces. This curiously encourages talk among our closer friends. Yeldig Notneff is a close friend and becomes a Jack. Randy Shaw, we think is cool—and whom I was still in love with distantly; I don't mind telling you that—at least as cool as us, and so we offer a position of Jack to him. So there are four Aces and two Jacks. Then there is Jack. The same Jack, who insists on becoming a Coolie. The wrong thing to do with the Coolies is to insist on anything. We have a meeting of the board (which means that we all look at each other and shrug) and report to Jack that the only post left within the Coolie hierarchy is the classification of Snot-rag. And so our friend Jack becomes a Snot-rag."

I am realizing that Matt is telling his story in first person present, and not past.

"The truth is," Matt continues, "organization threatens to make the Coolies a not-so-fun enterprise and we are afraid of disclosing the central, closely guarded secret of our gang, which is: there is no gang . . . We swiftly decide to limit the number in the gang, during an impromptu voting session in the school cafeteria, and to cut off any more requests for admittance. In the lexicon of the Coolies, we rationalize, there are only these seven positions. Only seven veils, only seven sins, seven wonders of the world; only seven samurai, and so there shall be only seven cool enough to rule in the annals of Coolie-ism. Only seven."

"How many?" I ask. Matt smiles like Harpo, then keeps talking.

He says, "This infuriates new kids applying for gangdom, and they demand to be indoctrinated into the non-gang. Any position that is available. Begging to be even below Snot-rag. Bringing a worried look to our faces. Because we are eleven we can't think of anything below a Snot-rag. We are white and middle-class (one is gay but closeted if that is possible at eleven).

"Teachers and parents want to know! What are all the students demanding! They are shocked to find out it is an interest in joining a gang.

" 'A gang in a suburb of Austin?' they sputter. 'Why, this demands immediate attention.' The Suburban Gentlemen agree.

"If anyone asks us what our gang does with our time, we make up some wild story just to see if anyone believes us. These stories are repeated from things that we hear real gangs do, or gangs that we see at the movies or on television. The real gang at our school is called the Stokes. The Stokes are three years older than we are,

1

have passed through puberty (something we have yet to do) and are kids that are from the other side of the tracks. (In Georgetown, there are actually tracks that split the community in half, and along with the richer people like the Mellons and the Ewings and the Morgans, there are the Brunos and Giapettas who live on the other side of the tracks.)

"Fortunately, we have a friendly connection to the Stokes. John H.'s sister is going out with Creighton Drury, one of the gang's leaders. We are safe. But not from the teachers."

This is a long story, I'm thinking to myself.

"Mr. B. picks John H. up from his desk, stands him in front of the class, and ridicules him until he cries. This gang business is not for Mr. B.

"As a matter of course, since the faculty is aware of our gang, they separate all of us Aces into four separate levels of education in our junior high school class. Jim is in D group. I am in C group. John D. is in B group. And John H., obviously the ringleader and the smartest, is in A group. Our scholastic aptitude is now affected because we are in a gang that doesn't really exist at all. We plead innocence, but history repeats itself. The Coolies are railroaded." Matt shrugs.

I wonder if he's the closeted gay in his gang, and concentrate more intently on his thick wrists, gesturing thus and so. Matt is getting into this story, as with other things (sex?).

He says, "Then to confound everyone, Reid Buckley, who is never allowed near us or our gang, and feels rejected, starts his own gang, called the Collies. This is a more democratic gang with a very unoriginal name that claims anyone who wants to become a member is to be allowed in and they don't have to be a Snotrag.

"So that is that, until one day on the bus I ask to become a member in Reid's gang, which starts a rumble with the Collies. Because there is something like fifty of them to three of us. We lose. But we give them that old Middlesex-John-Paul-George-and-Ringo try and make some of them cry because of our quick tongues, which cut deeper than their flying ring binders."

I watch Matt smile that Harpo Marx/Brad Pitt smile and take a sip of his China Cola while my mind uncontrollably drifts to another time, when *I* was eleven years old . . .

"Where are you going to place the camera?" Dewy Cyrus[45] asks me. (Dewy had shot everything that I have ever made.) "Where does the camera point? . . ."

A few clouds pass by the frame. Suburban lawn furniture fills the sky in an upper-middle-class surrealist motif.

I don't want to place the camera, I don't want to

---

[45] Dewy and Spunky have been making films together since they were in junior high school. Dewy is more contemplative and married to his work than Spunky is. He also resembles a great big bear, and nobody would mess with him when Spunky and Dewy were in high school because Dewy was so big.

work. I'm only eleven years old (a warm night wind, gusts) . . .

I remember the sudden realization that a moving body must make it through an infinite number of points in the vast area of a suburban living room, before it can reach its destination on the other side of the room in front of the television, or by the fireplace. And that those points could be recorded in some way.

Placing the camera is one of the most interesting parts of making a filmmercial. It is one of my favorite parts. Lately I have created a system of reacting to the presenter's performance in a camera-dance, a way of filming the scene that changes day by day and moment by moment, to try to capture the energy of the Now. I gather in a huddle with both videographers who help decide how to light and shoot the scene. A small story-board is sometimes drawn. Or I will shoot the first shot and then design the second. This is because the overall concept may change after Dewy has shot the first setup. Something may have occurred to me in the small inter-val between the last rehearsal and the end of the first take.

When I started making informmercials, the idea of creating its look as I went was too challenging, and I to-tally blew it. There was not enough solitude on a film-mercial set for me to make sound creative decisions. It was only later on that my method seemed to be working, although my crew looked at me pathetically, as if the "technique" of doing anything should be left at home with the dog and the kids. But I have no dog and kids.

The placing of the camera is something that one learns how to do patiently. It doesn't come all at once. It comes about after working for years, and even then it comes slowly. You slowly figure out there is more than one way to sell a potato peeler.

Screeching tires ripped up chipping asphalt from the mercilessly weather-beaten surface of the Stubtown airport. The tires and the asphalt made a comfortable scream in Blake's ears. He imagined how they might think about using a Titan 511 super-heavy-duty paver to lay down some new asphalt on that runway. Blake knew where to get one with an air-cooled six-cylinder Deutz diesel engine, three-point suspension and crawler chains with patented Lifetime® lubrication. He had never seen one up close, but he knew an outfit that was dealing them. Blake placed his tractor magazine face down in the seat next to him and zips up his personalized Cloudy-Bright Rehab duffel bag. The Lotus and L were not far now.

"I have been thinking about some of these off-market log loaders and stuff, L." Blake was pointing into L's reflective full-color dealers' catalogue from the Caterpillar corporation. Other catalogues were strewn across an unmade bed advertising sexy pictures of vehicles whose dimensional sizes started somewhere in the area of a small one-story house.

L shook his head. "I don't know about getting those models tonight, you did say that you needed them tonight?" Blake looked up at L, and L was holding an expression that said: I guess I didn't need to ask. He was beginning to feel the importance and the immediacy of such a buy.

"Oh . . ." Blake said, a sudden panic closing in on him tightening his voice. "I gotta have 'em tonight. Oh, it's gotta be, L."

"Now, don't worry, son, we'll get you something tonight." L looked over at Blake's companion, Li'l Chub, and shook his head as soon as Blake turned back to the full-color catalogue. "I'm guessin' Town Tractor has a few of them loaders."

"It's gotta be," Blake said, sticking his tongue between his teeth and just out one side of his mouth, concentrating on the next full-color page as he flips through the catalogue.

"Ooohhh!" he said, and pointed, "Now there are some real nice earthmovers, L."

"You're into movers now, that's pretty heavy stuff," L said.

"Them are beautiful . . . oohh . . ."

"Hey, Blake, what say we go pick up those three Cascade Log Loaders and head on out the ranch, then think about these cats later. Huh? It's gettin' kinda late here . . . and those loaders've gotta be beautiful, Blake."

"Don't rush me. I know when I'm bein' rushed, Li'l Chub."

"Okay, baby, I know, I know, but for expediency's sake."

"I'm not rushin'."

"Take your time, take your time . . ." L said,

"you gotta make sure you are gettin' what you want. Now these Japanese models over here . . ." L lifted a hardbound catalogue from his cheap Lotus hotel desk and curled the gooseneck light around to shine off the top of it. Gleaming into Blake's eyes was a brightly colored Japanese-made version of an Ingersoll Rand Static Tandem Compactor with 14 tons grade ability and a turbocharged 92-horsepower diesel.

"Not Japanese tonight, L," Blake grumped, "I want to get me some good old American machines. 'Fis okay witchoo." And after a quick look at the back of the catalogue, Blake looked up at L, the light from the gooseneck catching his watering Picasso eyes, darting back and forth between Li'l Chub and L. "You have any chain saws for sale?"

"Well, chain saws are plain easy, Blake, plain easy."

🌲

H ey, up there!"

No response.

"Hey, do you think that Felix's death was an accident?" I ask a man in the tree outside my house.

"Didn't you ask me that last week?" the man in the tree responds.

A dramatic wind rustles the pine needles in the tree, sending a spiral of them floating down on me.

Felix was in flight. He was in tune with the powers that are beyond us in a holy union of matter and electric light. "Life isn't a singular experience, it is collective, like atomic structures."

The first time that I met Swifty, he told me that Felix was an alien. Hmm.

The press seemed more pressed to find information that would shed light on "What happened to Felix?" He was just a kid. But a kid who could pick up a million dollars in a couple of months is no kid. There was more to be unearthed, something underground. Something buried underneath that politically correct facade.

They were repeating the question over and over again: "What really went on during the notorious shooting of the informmercial *101 Useful Things You Can Do with Flamex?*"

There was room for speculation. There were many rooms filled with people's speculations. And the tele-

1

photo lenses were aimed at those rooms now. In my house.

The gossipmongers and the scandal-sheet reporters were hovering outside my front door. There was something that I was hiding. There was something else to be told.

But what?

They began to make up the story for themselves, unsatisfied with the statements that I made.

Ordinary Joe: You just make up a story and make it happen, huh?

Reporter: Well, sometimes it's hard to find a good story, uh, so by the time you do all that work makin' it up, you don't want to let it go, you want to see it in print. So I say fuck it, if it's a good story, let it go to print, who cares if it's accurate or not. What's sellin' the paper anyway? Not accuracy, that's for fuck sure.

I remember a videocam whirred on my front lawn, brothers and sisters.

I spoke into a mike with "MTV" written on it: "He was one of the most beautiful people that I knew. I am completely shocked by the loss. Let me tell you something. I think that I knew him as well as anybody, and he was like all of us. He had a personal side of himself, and he had things that he did not like to talk about, but more than anyone, he was trying to find out about those things, and why you don't feel like talking about them.

"If there were any problems, he could have just as well talked about them with his friends, who he loved and who loved him just as much. I don't think there were any larger problems in the picture.

"It was just that there were aliens who were trying to take him into outer space. And he had made contact . . . with them . . ." I stopped myself and looked at the microphone with "MTV" written on it. I don't think that I was supposed to be saying this part. ". . . just before he disappeared . . ." I paused again, worrying that I was blowing it, looking at all the faces around me.

". . . on the Strip."

I had been visiting Joanna's workspace. She had a new editing setup and was showing me how the rapid rewind worked, the little electric engine whirring up the film really fast, when the phone in her office rang. She went into the office to get the phone and I looked around her studio. The office space was made of walls of what seemed to be scavenged wooden windowpanes of differing sizes, making a kooky framed-glass enclosure of about ten square feet. She leaned on her Macintosh computer and smiled to the person on the telephone line as if on a two-way videophone.

I tried rewinding some material on the new bench and the roll went spinning counterclockwise out of control, throwing my arm violently to the side and unspooling film on the floor. I stopped it halfway, causing the film to break with a great snap! I was cleaning this up when Joanna returned to say that we were going to go to Toad Hall to meet the reigning retrograde filmmaker himself, Buzz Post.[46]

The meeting place was dark, and had round wooden tables with inches of fiberglass finishing to make them impervious to flying chairs, broken glass or spilled col-

---

[46] Buzz Post, whom Spunky has quoted before, was the Sasquatch film community's hero. He was, or some thought, their Northwest Savior, having claimed his turf in the Hollywood Showbiz Media world with a few clean and savagely poignant dramas about life in the gutters of the city of Sasquatch. In fact his films always started out with a plain white title against black: SASQUATCH, OREGON. He was a passable force in the international independent film community, which was growing all the time. Spunky didn't know Buzz terribly well, but a lot of his friends thought that Buzz was a nice guy. There were a few people who said that he was a dick and was high on himself. And there were a few other people who said that he was confused and high on drugs. One of his old writing partners claimed to have been ripped off by Buzz. But that guy was a fake anyhow, so . . . when it came right down to it Spunky pretty much didn't know what to think of Buzz Post.

lege student brewski. Three of us, Joanna, Steve and I, sat by ourselves and waited for the retro king himself, Buzz Post, to show his passed-around face.

I called Buzz the retro king because most all of his films had retrogressive diners and cheap hoods from the sixties and seventies in them. I had seen the photos in magazines. He was once on the cover of a local newspaper, after he made his super-hit film *Looking for Lonnie*.

Buzz, of course, showed up late, and pretended that he had lost track of the time.

As if . . .

"How is everyone today?" he asked us, but I'm not sure if he really cared about how we were, it was just his opening line.

"I want to know what everyone is working on. You know, the stuff that you guys do is so interesting, eh?" he said, trying to fit in quickly and not realizing that he was being condescending. But where did he get that Canadian accent? He must have been shooting a film up there recently.

"I remember when we all used to sit at the Film Study Center in the old Masonic Temple building before anyone knew what they were going to do, and we were attending those useless seminars on film distribution with all the hopes young filmmakers have with nowhere to go but up, eh?" Buzz said.

The three of us look at Buzz. "We are still sitting in film seminars," I said but Buzz wasn't listening.

"Weren't those insufferable days, Stevie?" Buzz

1

slapped Steve on the back nostalgically as Buzz started drifting back into the seventies in a Toad-skin canoe.

"Hey, nice suit, Stevie, what is it?" Buzz asks.

"Ah, its 1995 Goodwill." Steve smiles and answers.

"Oh."

Buzz's clothing was seventies by design, but from Fred Segal in L.A., which only sells expensive designer Goodwill knockoffs. He wore an emerald-green metallic suit with a light green dress shirt open at the top, a tuft of chest hair fluffing out. No sign of drug use, by the way.

He leaned over the wood-and-fiberglass tabletop that was now spotted with squiggle-droplets of liquid and surprisingly asked me what I was working on.

I told him about a new Saber informmercial that I was in the process of pitching. "I'm trying to get Andrew Dice Clay to host a thirty-minute slot, Buzz," I said, sounding suddenly forceful, as if I were at a job interview. "Of course Andrew's agents say he's somewhat busy, they were sure Andrew would really like to talk about hosting the show, but I need to call them back in about two months. That's how busy he is."

"Mmmm . . ." Buzz buzzed.

"Anyhow, I hope that Mr. Clay will be interested. I am very encouraged, to say the least. But I am sure that although it is very exciting for me, it must be an almost daily experience for someone like yourself, Buzz." I gestured by tipping an imaginary hat on my head . . . and he smiled knowingly.

"Maybe I could help you get to Dice, pal," Buzz said.

"Oh, but you've got to be busy, Buzz," I responded.

"I know the Diceman, we play poker together sometimes," Buzz said. Joanna and Steve and I traded glances, hiding how impressed we were that Buzz regularly played poker with someone as famous as Andrew Dice Clay.

"I'll ask him about it," Buzz said.

Wow! Score!

"Hey, thanks, Buzz," I said. Maybe Buzz wasn't such an asshole like we thought that he was.

"Give me a call at home, pal," Buzz said, and wrote his number down on my shirtsleeve.

This changed some of my initial impressions of the guy right away. It was a brand-new shirt. Maybe he *was* on drugs. Yeah, now that I think about it, he's gotta be, look at him, he's practically falling asleep.

"Do you guys mind if I talk about myself?" Buzz asked.

Joanna tossed a disappointed look my way, then smiled and said, "No, Buzz, we want you to talk about yourself."

"I thought you might, which is why I asked. Are any of you aware of CD-ROM's potential in the marketplace?" he asked, pronouncing the ROM more like "Roam."

Of course Joanna and I both had worked on CD-ROM packages that were selling in computer magazines, but Buzz was unaware.

"I'm talking about the real shit," he swore, "honest-to-God moneymaking packages."

"I was unaware that our CD-ROMs weren't making money, Buzz," Joanna said with a little smile.

"Well, Mike Ovitz . . ."

Uh-oh. Here comes the name dropping.

". . . is going to get into this thing and it is going to be one helluva moneymaker . . . Disney! Can you picture it! Can't you see it, Steve? Joanna? Spunk? Biggest thing you could imagine.

"Why, they are already printing money over at Disney, but now . . . well, now they want to corner this CD-Roam market, boy, and I know that they can do it. And I want in on it," Buzz said as the waitress hovering over his left shoulder asked if Buzz wanted a drink. Annoying his enthusiastic temper, and momentum.

"Yes! Goddamnit. Vodka tonic, twist of lime, thanks. Anyone else?"

We held our glasses up to acknowledge that, one-two-three, we already had drinks.

"Okay then—you see the possibility of interactivity with their old releases? Snow White and the Seven Dwarf Stars? Cinderellogram? You see what I am saying?" Buzz effused.

"Seems like a job for someone over at Will Vinton's[47] . . ." Steve said.

"Enough said. It's going to be great, and I am talking to them about doing an original piece for exploitation," Buzz said as he tapped the table with his fingers, almost boring himself with however many times he had gotten wound up over this concept.

"Sounds great," I said.

[47] The man who registered Claymation®.

"It's great," Buzz said.

"Great . . ." Joanna said.

It was so great that it stopped the conversation. I could hear the cheese being grated right now, over the double pizza being prepared in the front window.

As far as I was concerned, Jack's movie and marketing ideas held a lot more water than Buzz Post's. Jack's conceptions are so new. I mean, Cowboy Nemo alone . . .

There are other movies that Jack has conceived. One he calls TEX*ASS, a story about Eddie and the good ol' boys who battle a small-town PTA and the quarterback of the team. Another called HAVE YOU SEEN MY RONNIE MOORE? and still another called L.A. CANNONBALL. CANNONBALL is about medical studies, movie extra work and a bowling habit. The lead character of L.A. CANNONBALL apparently has many names. Or maybe Jack means there are many choices for naming the character.

Jack says, "I mean that there are many different choices for names, but, like, maybe the character should go by a couple a different names, or there should be three names.

"Yeah," he says. "There should be three names, one name for when he is an amateur kid bowling champ, then anotha when he studies to be a doctor, and a new name for when he is a teen star, and then layta, another name when he develops a habit for bowlin'. They're nick-names."

There are yet other concepts, one is called THUN-DERMOUNTAIN, and others are called BRAND-NEW COWBOY HAT and THE LAUGHING DISTRICT. Where does he come up with these titles? He is a gold mine of them.

I sit in a park on a warm day talking with Jack and Matt about movie ideas.

Matt is wearing makeup today. Odd; looks good on him, though.

TEEN is an idea that is the center story of L.A. CANNONBALL. The cannonball is suggested by the cannonball-like appearance of the bowling ball. Jack was an amateur bowling champ when he was a kid in Georgetown. Jack says he ranked third-best amateur bowling champ, and the guy who was the first best had a nervous breakdown in high school.

"He could backspin the ball down the lane like an orbiting blue planet," Jack says. Something that Jack could never do.

I ask, "Is that the same time you attained the status of Snot-rag?" Jack squints and asks me if Matt told me that story. I have a picture of the young Jack in my head, looking just like the teenaged Felix, hair slicked back bowling style, multicolored bowling shirt with J A C K written on the back, sending the ball down the lane with a furious backspin.

The character of L.A. CANNONBALL has many

names, but Jack is beginning to call him Joey. Joey talks so fast that when he pronounces his name it comes out more like "Joy" than "Joey."

Joey tries premed at the University of Texas, but drops it in favor of breaking into the movie business. He moves to Movie-Town and gets work as an extra. This is something that I have tried before. I am relating. Eventually Joey attends Camp Hollywood, a place that teaches acting, continuity, memorization, lighting and blocking to young actors interested in being teen stars. Joey graduates and becomes a teen star briefly, then is attacked by a crazed fan who knocks him down. This is the TEEN section of the story. And later, Joey moves up to Sasquatch, Oregon, and finds an apartment across the street from a giant Bowling Alley called TIMBER! (Typical Sasquatch name for a Bowling Alley. There are bars, restaurants, amusement rides, all called TIMBER!) Joey is lured by the sound of bowling balls wafting through his apartment window. He takes to standing outside the ball reset area and listening to the falling pins. He develops an obsession for bowling, and spends all of his money on the game, eventually picking up games with people who will pay for him. Hustling bowling games.

Jack has worked on the other movie that he calls THUNDERMOUNTAIN (same name as Jimmy Keene's club in Vegas). It is something he says that Roger Corman might like to make into a movie.

Matt and Jack explain one of their pastimes is jumping onto the stage in punk clubs and grabbing the mike and singing impromptu lyrics or gibberish (or singing in tongues?) along with the band. They occasionally are thrown out of the music clubs for this behavior and are usually too drunk to feel any kind of remorse about it.

"The next day there is a kind of remorse," Matt says.

I say, "You mean that you feel sorry about it?"

His head lowers and he looks down at the ground with a somber little boy guilty look. I think that his front teeth have been knocked out and are now fakes.

"But," he says as he smiles, "it is worth all the guilt because some of the time the band really likes it, and you get to sing with a really great band like Stinky Puffs or Sebadoh, and they get off on it. It's worth it for that, they tell me."

Kids.

Later, in an Italian restaurant, Jack asks me about my childhood. I tell him I originally intended to be a painter. My eyes get distant. I look out the window of the Italian restaurant and listen to the music that is piped in.

I tell Jack, "Even at the age of thirteen I painted nearly all the time, spending less and less of it with my gang (I was in a gang like Matt's gang) in New Bedford, Connecticut. A very white-bread gang. I think that in fact we were actually dangerous and nobody realized it. Not even us. That's the thing about gangs.

"When I was with my gang, I remember one of the things that we did was dig in the ground to make an underground fort.

"My first foray into the underground. We would dig

out a four-foot-square hole and put wood on top of it and sit in there to talk and smoke cigarettes. The first time I exposed a piece of film, I was in the hole."

Jack seems mildly amused by this fact.

"I still have the picture of the square-shaped entrance at one end of the fort, and my friend Julian Falsetto is hanging from a tree limb. I remember that my father worried about the content of my pictures. (The last time that I exposed a piece of film, I also noticed that my father was worried about the content of my pictures, but he accepts it now because I am paid for it.) This was because they were mostly out of focus or so far away from their subject that the pictures began to look like routine surveillance photos that an insurance agent might make of a vacant lot before they put up a big building."

I think that Jack can relate to this. Or maybe he is nodding because he thinks the photos might have been good. In any case, he seems to approve.

"It is also when I first fell in love."

Jack looks at me.

"I was ten or eleven."

Jack looks away.

"With Julian Falsetto. He was very cute."

Jack looks back.

"And the attraction was never consummated, alas. Such was the fate of my intense attraction. I was too macho to risk anything. At age eleven in New Bedford, one didn't risk too much. When your father was a businessman in New York, you were encouraged not to risk too much."

Jack nods.

"But there he was, lovely Julian hanging from the tree. His muscular body draped over a tree limb in some unbelievably suggestive way, and then I would be in the hole, telling him that it was a really great shot. It was really a cheesecake shot of an eleven-year-old. I blush. It was really child pornography. Taken by another child. Does that still make it child pornography, or is it peer pornography?"

This makes Jack laugh (rare), and something that I notice that I am trying to make him do on purpose.

"Anyway," I said, "for me, there was a whole lot more going on than just an innocent shot of a kid in a tree. I was using the family Kodak™, a camera called a Pony®, which fit the situation perfectly.

"At the time, this camera looked like a very sophisticated piece of equipment. When I took a picture of, say, a squirrel in a tree, since I was too far away and didn't have a telephoto lens the picture looked like just a bunch of tree limbs. I was learning to see. My intention was for the picture to be a *National Geographic* squirrel portrait, or a *National Geographic* boy portrait. (The success of *National Geographic* being that for every sexual identity in the family there were sumptuous exotic and suggestive full-color pages of whatever your fantasy was, and existed in every bookcase of every middle-class family in America. That's America's hidden agenda.)

"My father thought I might be wasting film. He stopped me as I was replacing one of the latest issues of *National Geographic* in his library.

" 'I'm really into photography, Dad,' I said.

"He responded with 'Some good pictures in there . . .'

" 'Right.'

"He suggested that I make a list of the shots that I took. The processing of my photos was taken care of with my father's charge account at the local pharmacy. He thought that organization was the answer to cutting down on wasted, poorly composed shots."

Maybe Jack is bored by this. He is twisting his napkin into a long string.

"I never did get that organized. It was the hardknocks school of photography. About the same time, I play with a Brownie eight-millimeter movie camera and make crude stop-motion movies with troll dolls and my sister having tea parties with her stuffed animals. These little movies are made in the shadow of nearby New York underground filmmakers."

Jack tells me that his first influences were of the *Friday the 13th* variety. And also a film called *2000 Maniacs*. But later, when he saw *Eraserhead,* his influences changed. He says that hardly any of the films that he made back then make sense.

"My small films were so short there was no real pressure to make much sense with them," I say, "and besides, I was usually the only one watching.

"There are a few neighborhood friends who will

1

watch them but they couldn't have cared less about my film experiments. They don't understand that I want to change the way people watch movies. I am ambitious at this point in my life," I say. "I am thirteen.

"Julian Falsetto is still lurking in the corners of my daily life. I avoid him. I pretend that he doesn't exist, he is that distracting. But then we share a friend named Jack." Jack looks up from his project, where he has been making a very useful strong twine out of the paper napkin.

"Yes," I tell Jack, "the friend's name was Jack, a different Jack."

I get a creepy feeling. There are people walking by us on the other side of the restaurant window, it is midsummer and it is hot, which gives this reminiscence a somewhat ethereal feeling.

"When I am fourteen," I continue with my remembrance, "I have an English teacher named Mr. Kurtis Kay who wrote a hip schoolbook called *Stop, Look and Write*. He also does birdcalls and will show movies in our English class. Watching movies in English class is just a small step away from that schoolboy dream of being paid to watch television. By watching films, Kay has his students interested in making movies themselves. So it is that I make my first official film. I draw on pin-registered acetate a profile of a Victorian man's head. A little plant grows, tickling him under the chin. He bites the plant back to the ground. The camera pans over, widening our view to see more of the man's head, exposing that he too is growing out of the ground like a plant. He is a man/plant. Communicating some vague 'survival of the largest' or 'we are all of common soil' theme. The student who helps me film my first film is named Paul.

"Paul kills himself two years later when he is dumped by a girl he has been going out with named Mary. At the time I'm thinking Paul is taking his version of first love a little seriously.

"However, I show my first official film endeavor to a friend who has moved to Long Island. The soundtrack is a slowed-down seventy-eight record. When my friend leaves for Long Island he takes my new film with him, my only copy, to show his friends how clever I am. And although he means to give it back, he loses it. So my first film is completely lost, about three days after I have completed it. I have made no copy of it. Shit, that still pisses me off."

Jack laughs. He's bad.

With a crack over the head, I realize . . . "Jack, that's it! How temporary film is! As temporary as life itself! In my case it is because someone steals it and loses it. But there is certainly a questionable life expectancy of a film that might get lost, forgotten or turn pink with age. Pink again, Jack. Whereas flat art, Jack, seems to hang around as long as it doesn't get burnt up.

"Marshall McLuhan says that mass-produced items become rarer than things that are produced one at a time because the mass-produced items are expendable and are thrown away, Jack. Film is a mass medium and thus expendable.

"The way that a film is distributed is ponderous. Did

1

you ever notice, Jack? It is kept a big secret at first because the filmmakers don't want anyone else to steal their idea, then it is distributed and comes out all at once all over the country and people have a big discussion about it: which means they either like it or they don't. Then it makes a brief appearance (final curtain) on video. But then it is forgotten, and never really brought up again, except for nostalgic purposes. Just watch American Movie Classics on cable television and experience the nostalgia pour out. This excludes some lovers of film because for them film is an art."

This, though, strikes me as profound. My eyes begin to mist up. "Yes, Jack," I say, "climb up on a mountaintop and yell 'Art!' But for the general audience, film is an expendable transitory piece of cheap entertainment that focuses on the moment, and then is destroyed cruelly like drowning a little puppy after you are tired of playing with it. Once people have had a chance to see it, then that is it. Goodbye. How many times have you said 'I've seen that'? Which usually means 'I don't want to see it again.' It might even have been great the first time, but one is not sure that he has the time to burn watching something all over again. Time is precious to people and they try and save it. *Whatever saving time means.*

"I hope that my films will not be lost. But I don't have copies of them that I expect will last very long. It is up to the distributors who pay for them to take care that they don't get lost. I suppose videodisks do make one feel that the films will live out one's lifetime."

The conversation has completely turned one-sided.

I have been babbling and crying too long. Jack is looking at me as if I am a complete jerk. He looks as if he doesn't know what will happen next. Which is odd because we have been sitting in this restaurant over an hour. Maybe more.

Obviously nothing is going to happen.

Swifty lies invitingly at the end of my bed with his clothes off. I actually get laid now and then. He is teasing, shaking his butt around like he does, at the end of the bed. He has a long body, well muscled, with thick ankles and wrists that I like, and not too much hair, well, none on his chest. Black hair, or very dark brown. A perfectly proportioned chest, which I also like a lot. Strong shoulders and arms. And a big old scar that runs around his ankle. This is from a bungee-jumping accident.

He lies on his back and I fuck him, yes, we use condoms, with his nipples pointed upwards and his fuzzy round egglike balls chafing this way and that just under my belly button, wafts of penis smell drifting my way that drives me insane, Swifty and I, gasping in ecstasy as he is rubbing delicately on his penis until we both come at the same time. (!)

Or he will push me on my back and we do the opposite. I suppose you could consider it the missionary position for gay couples. For we were a couple. Way back. I miss him. He never calls, he is always out bungee jumping. I think that he has forgotten. He has a short memory. But I pine. I remember even though he doesn't. But I reserve these memories in the dustbin, or the closet, no, not the closet, the shelf, to keep for another day when he comes back to say hello, or some other young presenter that I might, perchance, become interested in.

Actually, it's not been that long since I have seen him. He is just passing through town with a circus act, Spike got him interested in circus performing, and even though he didn't call me when he got into town, we all went down to see him to say hello, and to wish him well. Because we all love him. Spike, J-D, Jack, Matt and I.

I tell him, when the circus is in town, we all come, because it is a small town, so here we are, deal with us. He laughs and is actually glad to see us, or so it seems. He stands there not knowing what to say, but there are four of us and we keep up the chatter. Swifty's hair is brushing the leaves hanging down from the limb of a tree we are sitting under. He is in good spirits, and we can hear nearby that he has quite a female following. There are young girls screaming for him from the side of the road by the circus tent. When he leaves, the girls say that they will pay twenty dollars for each leaf we can pull from the tree that they have seen Swifty stand under.

He says that he doesn't know how to deal with all the adoration because he hates himself so much. Swifty? I didn't know that he hated himself. That's distressing. But after we watch him perform a high-wire act (in white tights) he is off in the circus caravan before we know it, heading for the next town to do the wire act in, and make more girls scream. That's what his life is like now.

The buzzards screamed at me as I trudged down a dusty desert road on my way to the next screening at this remote film festival called the YUSA Fest. YUSA stands for Young United States of America, which this year is being held in an Arizona ghost town. I hope to run into some industry types who might be interested in my story $-GREAT SKULL ZERO-$.

Jack and Matt are here, amazingly enough. We have different passes, however, they are wearing the more expensive and exclusive pink passes that allow you to go to all the fancy parties and special events. I ask them how they got the pink passes, but their answers are elusive and vague.

Early one morning I attend one of the more (what I believe to be more) obscure screenings, a film called *The Sargossa Manuscript*. I arrive late, as a woman is talking about the history of this particular print we are about to see.

Apparently it was a film that the San Francisco counterculture would show in the Cinematheque in Berkeley, and became one of the best-loved of the time. The woman, who has gray hair, speaks fondly of the sixties, and of her youth. She says, "It is an indication of the kind of film we used to watch back then." Making the sixties seem so long ago. They are.

The woman tells us that the print we are about to see is a print that was made with much political maneuvering and many phone calls to Poland, where the negative exists. She says that Jerry Garcia said that it was his favorite film, and that he personally offered to pay to have the film printed, sent over, and donated to the Pacific Film Archives housed in the Berkeley Museum, a remnant of the Cinematheque. So I get the picture that these old countercultural figures from the sixties are curating their own history.

When the film was finally shipped to America, it arrived on the same morning that Jerry Garcia died, she says. Then the lights go down, and the film is shown. It is about the dead. Not the Grateful Dead, although perhaps that too, but it is about dimensional travelers who are ghosts or who are gone forever after they have died. It is a story within another story within a story within yet another story.

As I watch *The Sargossa Manuscript,* I hear one of the leading men say to a woman lounging on a veranda and feasting, "See you later."

And she responds, "Who can tell? . . ."

At the film festival I run into a few old friends at a huge barbecue in the middle of a small mining town in Arizona.

There is Brooke, who is a young gay boy from San Francisco, and happened to be passing through as he was wandering through the woods looking for adventure. And boys?

Then there was J-D, my ex-boyfriend and sometime assistant, picking up a hamburger from one of the party tables.

Heidi, who gives away the free shoes, this time at a film festival.

And there was Stewie again, the guy who at one time sued me during a disagreement over a filmmercial production.

Stewie is someone I am wary of.

Jack and Matt are attending with their special pink passes, which impress all of us. Perhaps they are showing their film, ha-ha. They must know someone at the top. Stewie is having a wonderful time, and tells me that he isn't like he used to be at all, that he has changed. I don't believe him. It is his way of trying to let me know that he *probably* wouldn't sue me again, but "probably" isn't good enough for me.

He is now more out of the closet than at the infovention.

He yells, embarrassingly loud, across a town street to J-D, "GUESS WHO I SLEPT WITH LAST NIGHT?"

J-D replies after he has bitten into a hamburger, "I know!"

Together, with their mouths full of food, they both say, "TIM!"

Jack and Matt were pretending not to listen, but I am sure that they thought they were next in line, and acted uncomfortable. I pretended not to notice.

At last we were at a gay barbecue together, with my gay friends and Jack and Matt. And in such a beautiful little town in the mountains. Matt puts his arms around Jack and kisses his ears and whispers something to him.

I ask Brooke, who is their age and gay, whether Jack and Matt are really that affectionate.

"No, it's just a fashion thing," Brooke says testily, "it's a post-Speechless thing, or a Green Day thing."

"Hmm. That's a good step, though, isn't it?"

Early in the morning I find myself having breakfast with Jack, Matt, Heidi and J-D. And the subject circles around something or another that has us talking about gay hippies living in rural places. J-D finds naked men with beards having sex with one another extremely distasteful. I am surprised at J-D. I tell him that he is homophobic.

But then J-D turns and point-blank asks Matt, "Are you gay?"

There is an uncomfortable pause at the table.

"J-D," I say, feeling proprietary, "what are you asking him . . . ?"

"Are you gay, Matt?" he asks again.

Matt says, "No."

I wonder if being a hippie has something to do with this question. As if Matt is a gay hippie because there are such things.

"I see myself as a single entity," he says. But with

some thought. I mean, it took Matt a little while to think it over. Wondering to himself exactly how he is.

J-D is on it, in a Dutch way of course, and asks, "Then you are asexual?"

And Matt responds, "Yes."

How uncomfortable all these questions and answers are. Jack and Matt are twenty-two years old. I mean, I know they are not teenagers, and they should know the answer to these simple questions, but do they have to be asked at the breakfast table with a bunch of strangers around? I suppose that they do.

When I return from the film festival there are new tire tracks burnt into the lawn outside my home. I decide that I cannot take the punishment of tire marks any longer and I stay up late nights holding a camera loaded with special night film and a strong flash to catch the person who is driving over the grass.

I wait a whole week for them to come back, and when they do, I am ready.

One early morning I hear tires spinning on the lawn strip outside and I wake out of a light sleep. I grab my camera and start running out to the front lawn just as they are stuck up on the curb. There are four of them, all in white T-shirts and driving Mom's car. They can see me running toward them at full speed. The little ones in the back seat are yelling at the driver to hit the gas. Then I take the picture.

It is a fantastic picture. There is one panicked back-seat fourteen-year-old screaming at the driver and the boy next to him looking over his shoulder to see what's going on, and a license plate nicely positioned in the corner. Aries, the make of the car, is visible in the other corner of the picture, perfectly situated and lit in an almost planned Jeff Wald[48] composition, the strobe of the flash catching the tense early morning moment in a beautiful still life.

They are just youngsters in Mom's car, like J-D thought. He is so wise sometimes. They aren't threatening, but cute, just making a little trouble to amuse themselves. Indiscriminate vandalism for a laugh. It would be painful to try to get them in trouble for it. They look too innocent. Too domesticated to reprimand.

I forget about the whole thing and they quit running over the grass in front of my house. Now I miss it sometimes. It feels like they don't care anymore. Have they forgotten me? It was one of the few real-life dramas I had going and now I've brought it to an end by scaring them with my camera.

※

[48] A world-renowned Vancouver, British Columbia, artist who uses photography in his pieces.

Blake was beginning to dwell on some of his past mistakes.

But who said that he should dwell on past mistakes? His past which was beginning to look to him like it was made up of nothing but mistakes. He didn't have to dwell on those mistakes right now. Now that he had decided what to do about it. He needed to tend to his future mistakes now.

He loaded his newly bought Tecumseh chain saw into the blue leatherette trunk of the family Camry and drove out to the country ranch that he was ashamed of owning. The ranch seemed to him an extravagance that only a rich city person would have, and growing up poor, he hated rich people. But now he had to face that he was one of them. One of the rich. But he was going to take care of that.

The Camry bobbed and bumped on the country road leading around a rocky hill that had three juniper trees on it, to the back of the property. Li'l Chub was going to come along with Blake to the country property, but Blake decided he wanted to be alone in the woods with his machines. He said he was going to write songs.

Blake began a rundown of the things he wanted to write Blackie and little Bill, Binky and Bartholomew, and for that matter, his public. Who should be duly notified about his thoughts. Talking to his public was something that he wanted to do. Darn, he was obliged to. They should know what he was thinking although he didn't think that they were going to like it.

He was sitting in the driver's seat of his Camry holding a pen in one hand and keeping a piece of paper flat over the air bag in the middle of the steering wheel. His mouth was open in a long hysterical crying jag and his drool was stringlike as it came slowly out of his mouth to fill the folds in his worn-out jeans. He hadn't written a word, but had been sitting there just like that for almost an hour.

He sucked air into his lungs with a violent jerk, then dry-heaved the last few breaths of his long cry out again. He could just barely breathe like this.

A small rabbit jumped when it heard the sucking-air sound of Blake's next breath. It stopped, its ears popped up and it looked to the Camry that had its lights still on. Blake's figure opened the door of the car, he stayed like that for a minute, and then he got out. Making the little rabbit run for its life.

Wind was howling through the trees as a large road grader was making its way over a hill with its lights on. It was being delivered by L into a large circle of behemoth vehicles that were filling a small valley on the property. The grader was a prized vehicle for Blake, he liked this one best of all. It had an air-conditioned cab, so that no matter how much dust you kicked up, you were safe inside the cab listening to your eight-track.

Blake was never happier than when driving his heavy machinery around his place.

Blake walked up in the woods firing up the chain saw and he started cutting wood. But he'd just as soon let his mind drift and embrace the noise of the saw and, in its punk rock enthusiasm, a scenario of suicide that had to do with the chain saw, and his neck.

Blake coolly devised a fantastic levered system to allow the chain saw to lower onto his neck after he had surrounded himself with the rest of his largest tractors after L had left.

There was a thick master rope which held the weight of the saw, and allowed it to be maneuvered up and down by two smaller ropes tied to tubular handles crisscrossing the body of the chain saw.

Blake pulled the rope, and suddenly the contraption jumped and the thing started cutting into one of the metal tubes that had slipped from the handle. With a great snap, the chain flew off and wiggled over Blake's shoulder like a canned snake.

He used a flashlight to try to repair the damaged chain, but there was a link missing, so he threw the whole thing into the dumper of the gigantic road grader and walked off down the hill.

The bunny rabbit ran after him, but not on purpose, it was just the way the rabbit run went.

A deer saw the light go on in the dirty little room off the main house where Blake kept his guns. The deer, who was nibbling on a firm tuft of sagebrush, could see Blake's figure moving around under a bare lightbulb, then settle out of sight near the floor of the room.

Inside the dirty room Blake wrote a note:

To Bra-Man corrected,

I don't want to seem like I'm complaining, but I think that you'll get my drift. All my Orlando backup singers have tried to tell me over the years that since the introduction to my first road grader they have watched me fall away from the simple enjoyment of playing and singing at a concert.

Now, I'd just as soon tell 'em to fuck off, but I have been noticing that I'm not fooling anybody at the shows. I play as if I never fuckin' learned how and now I'm scared shitless that you guys can tell. I feel overcome with a sense of grief at what I see staring back at me in front of the stage. Hundreds of lost young faces that are there just to hear my major chords and primal screams. And that's not what it's about.

Gosh darn! Why don't I keep playing? I don't know.

My three sons remind me so much of my fucked-up self that it scares me. I can't face them becoming the butt rocker that I have become.

Oh, I hate myself. Oh, I don't know. Thank you for all your help and all the tickets you bought.

Love, Blake

Bill, Binky, Bartholomew and Blackie, I'll be by your side, please build the road without me . . .[49]

When he wrote the last word the gun was already in his mouth. And Blake pulled the trigger. He was smiling and thinking of Ernest Hemingway when he did this, and he was going to be happy soon.

---

[49] This last comment confused Blake's cryptographers, for he had never mentioned a road to anyone except that one time to Blackie, who had forgotten he had said anything about a road. But one day it flashed across her mind as she read the note. "He was going to build a road," she had realized, and issued a press release that was forty-nine pages long talking all about the road. The mystery had been solved, sort of. Still nobody knew where he would go on the road he wanted to build. "Perhaps," the cryptographers surmised, "it was a symbol."

The gun made a sound, buried into his mouth, shoved up against the back of his fleshy palate, but it was not a bang. It was more like "punk." It was definitely that short, muffled and so appropriate sound . . .

"Punk."

I am thinking about aliens, brothers and sisters. "We are aliens," Felix said. "They are us.

"Aliens are not beings who come from other planets. The aliens are us," he had said, "and they are from another dimension, not another planet, and they desperately want to talk to us, but they do not allow themselves. Unless they are illegal aliens."

"Why, these apparitions happen all the time, and people aren't aware of them," Lewis Loving[50] was saying.

"It is extreeeemely common. It-is-just that you have to let yourself receive-the-vision, and allow-it-to-live. People don't want to be seeing things all over the place, they want everything nice and simple. Nice and simple. And so they don't see anything!" Lewis droned on.

"Did you know that time has been going backwards since last Tuesday?" a girl asked.

I recognized her. She was the pretty girl at the Felix Arroyo Corningwear™ book signing in Las Vegas. As far as I was concerned, time had always been going backwards

---

[50] Lewis Loving is a local unprinted author of some renown. He publishes his own material on a Xerox machine and has a devout following in Sasquatch. He is also full of paranormal information.

and forwards at will ever since I was a four-year-old and fell off the preschool slide in Denver, Colorado, at twelve-fifteen on March 9, 1948 . . .

One time she had hitchhiked up to Sasquatch, apparently to see Felix, and on the info set I had given her a bowl of tomato soup. At the time I hadn't noticed any of these apparently schizophrenic tendencies. Those were new.

I am not a psychologist, but as a nonpsychologist I was accustomed to identifying different nervous conditions of people around me . . . epilepsy, narcolepsy, St. Vitus' dance, sociopathy, cerebral palsy or Tourette's disease. These were more than general pedestrian medical conditions.

"At the corner of Market and Castro streets, I noticed that time started going backwards," she said. "I did some drawings. Do you want to see them?"

I stopped to think. If I looked at the drawings, would I be complying with her delusions? Are the drawings about time? And did I *have* time to look at the drawings if they were about time?

The drawings were folded up in little tiny squares and took about a minute to unfold. There was a group of people hovering around us, expecting some kind of show.

When the drawings were unfolded, well, I knew that I had diagnosed the general symptoms of schizophrenia fairly closely.

Time was certainly going someplace in these drawings. Mostly, I feared, it was being wasted. She seemed satisfied with my perusal, and then folded the drawings back into impossibly tight little squares that looked like pieces of wrapped chewing gum and disappeared. I haven't seen her since that time, but lurking in the back of my mind is the feeling that I will, at another time.

There was a time when my parents and I were discussing what would have happened had my mother, who almost married Roy Brown Hale, did marry him.

"I would have been different," I suggested. "I would have had a different last name, for one thing, and I would have perhaps looked different."

But my parents disagreed.

"You wouldn't have existed at all," they said to my falling eight-year-old face.

"Someone else would have existed."

"But I would have been that someone else, Mommy."

"No, dear, you simply would not be here at all."

I could not conceive of it.

"What would have happened to me?"

"We don't know, dear."

They didn't know, but they also were confused that they didn't know. I would have apparently been unborn. Nothing.

. . .

Jack and I are getting really chummy now. He accepts me. Jack wants me to meet him and he wants to give me something. I ask him what it is and he says it's a package.

"Well, what is in the package?" I ask.

"Something that I want to give you," he says, "black-and-white stuff."

"Oh," I say, "is it the screenplay?"

"No," he says.

What the fuck is it? This is so kooky, all these mysteries with them.

"I tried to find you downtown. I knew that you had a meeting with a Dutch distribution representative for your Flamex filmmercial account," he says. "I didn't know where you were meetin' but I thought that I might run into you someplace."

He thought that he could find me without communicating, like radioing in on me or something. Maybe it was a test of some sort. To see if I would actually show up on their screens. Very weird.

And there are two new script ideas that Jack wants to write, one is called CAT CALENDAR. Tell me that isn't weird.

Now, before Jack writes these screenplays, he is going to go take a job as a production assistant on a television show. The same one that Luke Perry is starring in, *Beverly Hills 90210*, that's the name of it. It makes sense that Jack works in Hollywood, the way he seems to know all those glamorous H/wood people and everything. He's probably writing episodes for them in his spare time.

Jack also mentions that the lead actor in his film *Don't Leave Me Georgetown*, which he is constantly shooting but is apparently unfinished, has dropped out of the project because of a bad back.

Poor old Jack is going to have to find another lead now. Or just face the fact that the film is already finished.

Dear Brutha,

I been really gettin' inta this film thing. It's awesome. I been figurin' that what I really need is a star in tha thing. I'm buggin' to go to Hollywood to see if I can get anyone innarested. Maybe some young teen star would do it. I don't know.

One of my actors dropped out with a bad back. I hope he gets betta. It is real hard just to get everyone together to shoot. When I started this film I didn't know that filmmaking was so hard.

Wait till you see yourself in it, you are going to trip.

peace, Jack

Πινκ αλτ. υνιϖερσ.

I have nothing to do. This is the number one personal problem that I have to deal with while I am on the inside. When I have nothing to do, I find myself shopping for more machinery. Even when I know it isn't going to change this feeling that I have nothing to do, and I already have seventy-five vehicles that I don't operate anyway. So one thing I have to work on is feeling calm and in control when I don't have anything to do. To be happy with nothing to do. Or to be satisfied that the world isn't going to end when I don't have something planned out to do. The other antidote to this condition is to find something to do. To start doing something. Just about anything will do the trick. Instead of crying about having nothing to do, I have to do something about it.

I have nothing to do. Or is it that I don't want to do anything. Is it a secret desire I have, to do nothing? Doing nothing seems more like really nothing at all than even taking a vacation. I don't go anyplace special. I don't read anything of importance or create anything worthwhile. I am really just wasting my time, like waiting for a bus.

I am waiting for an idea to hit. An idea as big as a bus. One that is big enough to transport me and my ideas through a major project that will take months to complete. Really my business is so inconsequential that I may as well not do it. But without a task in front of me I will just coast. Until I am inspired. I wonder if other info artists operate in the same manner. I decide to not feel guilty about it, and decide doing nothing is a good thing and not a bad thing.

Inside the Rubber Neck Grill one morning, I am delicately handed sensitive information that alarms me. Joanna has heard that Matt and Jack are from another dimension.

"Really?" An alarming suggestion.

She too has seen the film of Cowboy Nemo, the one that I have yet to see which Jack said he wanted to talk about. They apparently travel in other dimensions regularly. I ask Joanna how she put this info together.

"I had been in the group of neighborly potluckers who had expected a rapture. Jack and Matt had gone away, and when they are away, we assume they are traveling in them, in the dimensions," she says.

I don't want to believe it at first, but this is starting to make sense.

"I don't want to suggest that they go away in the sense that they are away for a length of time," she corrects herself. "They are away in another dimension, but it doesn't take any time."

Joanna keeps her cool and speaks in a low voice. This could be front-page material.

My concern over my next filmmercial all of a sudden becomes a very distant one. It is as if I am no longer a filmmercial maker. They, the Two, Jack and Matt, are suddenly more important than work. They moved from their old apartment and I don't know where they live. Maybe they live in another dimension and don't need an apartment. But that is silly, Spike has been over to their new apartment.

Spike? I haven't seen Spike in a while.

They are dimensional cowboys. They are Cowboy Nemos.

They have become well known around town and already several people that Jack and Matt have been talking to have surprisingly agreed to go with them into the other place.

"They call it Pink," Joanna says. "I am going with them, Harris, René, Julius, Jules and some others."

"Harris?"

"Yes, Harris too."

"They are called the Two?" I ask. "I thought they were student filmmakers."

"That's what they want you to think," she says, "but they aren't."

"Perhaps all the stories they have been writing and talking about is their way of talking about dimensional travel without spilling the beans," I say. "Perhaps the Cowboy superheroes are supposed to be them. And they have been sucked into another dimension to learn about their superpowers." It is too disturbing to think about. "Could this be it?"

Joanna slowly nods her head up and down. "Yes. It is the end of the Universe as we know it."

I have to talk to Jack.

Jack is talking a mile a minute about Drew Barrymore, a teen star. For right now Jack is obsessed by her.

He wants to put her in his film.

"She's got the Barrymore family name," he says, "and they were all on tha edge. There's even a movie I saw, a really awesome movie, called *Broadway's First Family* or somethin', dat's not the title; Fredric March plays John Barrymore and there's Ethel Barrymore and there's, um, the mom, I think Ethel was the sista. I think Lionel is in there. But John shows up and he's a really wild dude. He has a gigantic llama coat on, and he has a broken hand, and he is runnin' from the law, and tha way that he decides he is goin' ta run away is by goin' on safari in Africa. He is runnin' because he hit a film directa in the mouth on a set, and he is afraid that he is going to be put in the Joint, because he has done it three or four times before."

Jack talks even faster, saying, "It was a film that was about a sort of royal family who lived and worked on Broadway. An irresponsible royalty. Sort of like our rock and roll royalty of today, fucked and irresponsible and selfish and way tuned into themselves and so tweaked about it with their heads so far up their asses that they ain't never going to get beyond their own music and press. With followers that just feed that predicament, like an old royal court.

"Same thing as the old courts, with the jesters and confidants, and squealers and yes-men and money and shit. Fuck. The sort of Barrymore legacy stretched back before the twenties, the parents of the Barrymores I think were Broadway actors in the 1800s, so then they were the kids and so their legacy was like the Kennedys of Broadway and here's little Drew who is the grand-daughter of John. I don't know her but the legacy of her grand-pop is pretty amazin'.

"One story I heard was about John propped up dead at a goodbye dinner with his drinkin' buddies, nothin' but a corpse, and they are all havin' dinner and drinking and toasting good old goodbye John. Fuck. I mean it was kind of like Sinatra and the Rat Pack. But even Sinatra wasn't as tweaked. John Barrymore isn't really a controlled human. I mean in a way. He was a great artist. I lived in Lionel Barrymore's house when I first moved to Hollywood. It was called the Eagle's Nest. It was on a street where there were other famous movie star houses, like the Wolf's lair, etc. Real Hollywood Beverly Hills bullshit, fake sensationalism, fake royalty."

Is Jack losing it?

He says, "Lionel Barrymore built the Eagle's Nest. You gotta hand it to them, they knew how to hype themselves, and they knew how ta time-travel. With their old funky movies.

"All these famous time travelers in the twenties sitting up in their fantasy dream castles shooting pool and drinking Pernod. There were apparently famous pool games in the poolroom, which was used as a storeroom when I lived there. But, you know, W. C. Fields was a crony, so you have trouble right there. And there were other well-known drinkers."

Jack begins to slow down, and says, "It always was weird, because you were there where it happened, in the same room, but it was in the past."

Funny but I have never heard Jack talk about the past before. Why doesn't he just beam himself back there if he is so interested?

He continues, "Sometimes late at night, if I smoked

some pot and listened carefully across the canyon from my little guest house, I swear I could hear pool balls cracking in the poolroom and a W. C. Fields voice saying, 'Lionel, my boy, if I only had a' . . . and fading away . . . 'Same ol', same ol' . . .' "

Pink

Πινκ αλτ. υνιϖερσ.

Inside of a broken-down mansion in the daytime there are chips of marble coming up from a meeting-room floor. A long Alan Parker dolly shot close to the ground as in the movie version of Pink Floyd's The Wall. *The dolly shot examines the chipped marble for seemingly no reason except that it looks really cool when the camera is that close to the ground. It really does. We finally arrive at feet. There are many feet. They are sitting in a circle. The feet are bathed in a strong window light streaming Alan Parker-ishly all over the place, with a slight fog filter, perhaps a no. 1, giving it just the right diffusion. We may even have taken the daylight correction filter off of the camera so that the window light is very cool and blue. A young black man with dreadlocks stands in the group and says, "Hello, I am Benjamin—I am an alcoholic and cross-addicted." The group, which we can hear more than we can see, all speak in unison to welcome Benjamin: "Hello, Benjamin!" Then Benjamin finishes: "I know how to get clean and sober, please help me to stay clean and sober." Then another stands in an Alan Parker homage to Leni Riefenstahl, which is unusual for Alan to do, which only makes it that much better. "My name is Jerry—I'm an alcoholic and cocaine addict." "Hello, Jerry!" "My insides are not like my outsides, please help me to change myself." And another: "I'm Ha-*

1

reem—I'm a crack addict." "Hi, Hareem!" "Please help me to recognize my problems." So while this is happening credits are being presented over the introduction.

Cut to same place but a little later as one of the inmates is describing something he has thought about in his past. He is near tears. (Credits continue to appear: Production Designer, Director of Photography . . .) "I cried when I was sitting in front of the television and there was this cartoon . . . you know, the one with the coyote . . ." Another inmate speaks up as he is staring intently at Hareem, relating, "Wile E. Coyote," he says. "Yeah, Wile E. Coyote, and he's chasin' this bird, and I'm sitting there and I realized that no matter what happens to this coyote, he's getting mashed with the rock (view of coyote getting mashed with a rock) . . . shot into space (likewise, the coyote is shot into space). Blown up (credits continue over explosion). Flattened. Hammered . . . I realize that is me . . . I am the coyote—and the bird . . ." another inmate speaks up: "The roadrunner." "Yeah," Hareem says, "the road . . . roadrunner, yeah, right on. The roadrunner is the drugs. And no matter what happens to me I'll still try and get the drugs, like Wile E. Coyote, and that realization made me cry." A counselor breaks into the discussion: "Okay, what we are concentrating on is what makes men cry." The counselor has long fingers, and he looks at all the eyes in the room to establish contact. (The last credit fades up on the

screen: A film by Alan Parker.) The counselor fin-
ishes his thought: "And whether that is acceptable, or
whether men are allowed to cry in our society. Re-
member the topic."

Δ

When I get ahold of Matt he senses that I am anxious. He thinks that it is my time. My time to know. (?) He begins to talk about things obliquely. He includes in his ramblings a reference to Pink, referring to dimensional travel as Pink.

When he had told me that his father was writing a story called *Pink,* the buildings that his father was referring to are substitutions for rooms outside our dimension. And his father, he says, is a substitution for an outside presence. Like God.

"In the Pink/In God." And "pigs" is a code word for us. For human beings. Pigs?

Are these aliens, feeling like superior aliens? Matt? . . . what is Thundermountain, besides a nightclub?

Felix had gone out one night to Thundermountain with his girlfriend. He had brought his guitar along to play with the house band at the club. And before he knew it, he was dancing around the dance floor imitating John Travolta in *Saturday Night Fever.* He was sweating and looked like he had a fever.

There were many other teen spokesmodels there that evening. And they were all dancing too, although nobody really recognized Felix, because he looked so much different in person than he did on the informmercial screen.

He started feeling sick, and his brother and his sister took him outside to get some air. And what happened after that was he collapsed in the gutter outside Thundermountain.

There was a photographer there with a bunch of cameras around his neck but he didn't feel like taking any pictures, because the scene was too shocking.

The other presenters and spokesmodels there were hanging on the sidewalk, in front of low-riding Chevrolets with their radios turned up high.

Felix's sister was sitting on Felix's stomach because he had begun to convulse there in the gutter. And she saw a light go out of his eyes. Slowly his body, which was between her legs, began to go cold. And she knew they were losing him really fast.

His heart was no longer beating. And his little brother, who was calling the ambulance, and who was checking in on him every few seconds, saw this too, and it was all very horrible, and all very too late for any kind of help.

And that was it. Jimmy Keene[51] was standing there with his girlfriend, and noticed that Felix's legs were delicately crossed at the ankles, even after all of that thrashing around.

---

[51] Jimmy Keene was the second most successful and charismatic young teen spokesmodel in Las Vegas, next to Felix. He wore a lot of jewelry, had a great smile and movie star good looks. Jimmy Keene owned a huge casino on the Strip known as Thundermountain. There were suggestions that Jimmy had ties with the mob, but there were never any arrests to suggest this kind of thing was true.

. . .

Jimmy says, "I consider ourselves members of a world that includes all the creatures on earth, and those of us who place human beings on the top rung of the ladder above all the other creatures, well, I have a problem with that. I don't think that we are on the top, if you consider all the messed-up things that humans are capable of . . . There are other places to be and things to be part of, and it was just Felix's time to go and be a member of that new place. I don't look at the place that we go after we are alive as a bad place. It is a great place."

Felix had had violent seizures outside a hip Las Vegas club frequented by young presenters, and had fallen into full cardiac arrest in the ambulance that was transporting him to the hospital at one-thirty in the morning. All the tabloid press wanted to know was about drug use. Felix was an inexperienced drug user.

Maybe it was the mob. Maybe they did it.

"It just kills me, you can rip open my chest and vomit into it," Jimmy Keene said to the pulp showbiz press at the time.

He had some sort of contact that the rest of us do not have. He might not have known what it was, but he had it. He left us at the age of twenty-three, which, according to Bob Tobbins,[52] is the most used number when disasters or revelations occur.

[52] A well-known Everglades numerological writer.

Oh-no.

"Look, you get older or you die. Felix died, he won't be getting older. His youth will live forever, because we never will have the chance of seeing a seventy- or eighty-year-old Felix lounging under an orange tree on his estate in Peru," Spunky said. "It is not a continuing story. He didn't call. He left the party. He never surfaced . . . he turned blue on us . . ." Spunky lowered his head.

"So what else . . . ?" I can remember Felix saying to me over the phone as we talked. "So what else . . . ?" meant that we had talked about his latest commercial, what he thought about the destruction of the rain forests, my next informmercial, music we had heard that we liked, updates on his group of friends that he left up in Oregon after the shoot of *101 Useful Things You Can Do with Flamex*. I'm forgetting what his voice sounded like.

"What else . . . ?" he would say, as if he were being distracted by something. So I would tell him a story about something that happened to me that day, or something current that was happening in Sasquatch politically or personally. He was *very* interested in one's personal life—so he could relate his own personal life.

I remember Felix was sharing a double hotel suite with a couple, once saying, "They stay in their room all day screwing and they make so much fucking noise!" He laughed. "I mean, it is so fucking distracting. I don't make that much noise when I fuck, do you? I mean, like, I don't go: 'OH, BABY!!! FUCK ME!!! FUCK ME!!!' I'm more like [makes a sound like a strangling chipmunk], like that," he said.

He would know the fifteen varieties of how people "do it." Largely because he would have to "do it" in an informmercial and would have fifteen ways to choose from—one that would fit the presenter he was playing.

"What else . . . ?"

"Nothing else, nothing I can think of.

"Hey, if anything happens to me, I will find out a way to contact you, like if I die or something. I'll find a way to come back." I felt a little spooked out when he said that.

"Okay, then, I'll talk to you soon," I said.

And he would too. It must have been the same way for Felix's other friends. He would just say, "Hi . . ." and you would know who was calling. Sometimes the call would last only twenty seconds.

"Hi," he said. "Are you sleeping?" he said the last time that he called.

"Yeah," I said.

"Go back to sleep. I'll call again."

He hasn't called again. I will miss the calls that went . . .

"Hi, it's me."

"Hey."

"Hi, what's happening, Spunky?"

"Nothing."

"Tell me something . . ."

"Okay, uh, yesterday I went out with J-D . . ."

"Oh, J-D, what a crazy jerk . . ." Which meant that Felix liked J-D.

"What else?" Felix would say; a pause, and he would whisper again, just like Jack, "What else?"

"Well, could you tell me how time became unstuck, and how I meet up with a guy who looks just like you, called Jack, who likes to go 'in the Pink'?"

Where are they anyway and how come I went back in time so quickly?

"Pink" sounds like a term that Jack and Matt are using to refer to the unexplainable.

"It is a label for the dimensional travel that we are part of. It is a large part of what we are," I am finding out.

"It is so alien a dimension that there is no way that you can understand what it is," they explain to me.

"Oh."

"But Pink is easy to understand once you go there or are in it," or whatever it is they tell me that you do with it.

"You experience it," Jack says. "It is like trying to explain a doily to a dude who has never seen one, and then when they see it, it is awesomely simple."

"Is Pink like a doily?" I ask Jack.

He turns away and shakes his head and says, "No, man." He is unable to explain.

Πινκ αλτ. υνιϖερσ.

*Inside an Alan Parker film again, inside of the inside.
Window light. So much of this window light, where
do they get it all? Another small group is sitting in a
circle. It is a group that is made up of men and
women. A small black woman breaks the silence.
"Don't forget that what you hear in the group is con-
fidential and you cannot repeat it out of group. It stays
in the group. Now who can tell us their story? . . .
Let's see . . ." Her eyes scan the room over seven young
black men and women and one white guy, me. "Dara?
Would you tell us your story?" I lean closer. Dara begins to talk. She is hesitant, because it is hard. "I grew
up in the Bronx and lived with my mother and my father." The Alan Parker look reflects off of her black
skin as she touches her face with her left hand, and
sometimes cups her eye in her palm. The image of her
mother and her father seems to have registered, and
she is shocked to find herself back there. It is suddenly
real, and she is like a little girl again. And everyone is
listening. "I had a sister." The image of her sister is
clear to her. "And both my mother and father were al-
coholics. They didn't pay attention to me. I would go
to school and sit by myself in the class, and at home
my mother and father wouldn't talk to me. They were
drinking. And little by little I started to drink too.
Sneakin' drinks. And then I was drinking at school.
And sometime later, I checked into Detox for the first*

time. I was in a hospital." Dara begins to talk in short breaths because she is remembering so much. "And I got me some pills." She stops here, maybe because the pain of remembering is great, but I am not sure. It makes for a dramatic moment. "And I swallowed all of 'em. I tried to kill myself. Next thing I knew I was getting my stomach pumped of the pills. That happened two times." The group is silent. Most everyone is looking at the floor. Some are looking at their hands. After a moment the counselor breaks in: "Now, can we get some feedback about Dara's story, who can give us some feedback?" A hand raises. "You don't have to raise your hand." "I'm Tyler and I'm a crack addict." All respond, "Hello, Tyler." "I didn't hear about her parents, that was kinda passed over. Did you talk with your parents?" Dara is frozen. She shakes her head slightly side to side. Someone in the group announces, "She shook her head no." Karl raises his hand. "Hello, I'm Karl and I'm an alcoholic and cocaine addict. Dara, your story affected me very much. I think that the most serious thing you were talking about was your suicide attempt." Dara's face changes and she begins to cry. "Two times?" Karl asks. "How many times?" Dara says, "Two . . ." Then Dara really begins to cry loudly. The counselor breaks in: "It's okay. It's okay." And then there is a silence as the whole group witnesses Dara's tears pouring down her cheeks. Others in the group begin to cry with her.

The counselor looked about the room, and saw an

older man who was dressed in bib overalls who looked like he came from the country.

She said, "Nikita, could you share anything with us?" And Nikita moved in his seat a little and moved his head a little and said, "Oh, I've got some secrets. One, she didn't know about the pigs. That is one thing that she didn't know about. There's got to be an explanation about her not knowing about those huge round-shouldered dream pigs. She wouldn't acknowledge them. And she also wouldn't acknowledge a little indiscretionary problem I developed. Sometimes I think that she used the pigs as a physical or a dimensional manifestation of my indiscretion. We were all farmers out in the country outside Minsk, and the only people that we knew were farmers. Farmers and their farmer wives and their farmer kids. And every book we read and every movie we saw had farmers in them. They were doled out in cheap distances, I mean amounts. Because everything we had was doled, given, to us, like. Did you get yours now? Did you get yours last week? Are you getting any? These were things we asked ourselves every day of the week. All in good faith. And in good time the pigs and the canaries took a Sunday walk—that is, they died. I traveled to Minsk to see if I could find any replacements. Up Minsk-ways I would stand transfixed as I stared at the girl who began hummin' to her pigs. First time I ever saw any girl who was not a farmer. She wasn't. She was hummin' to 'em, and I was ankle deep in a pond filled with detective magazines. Oh, I would say that I have some secrets. Yes I would." Nikita from Minsk began to slightly rock back and forth, and said, "Well, I got to know her, yes I did. And she was no farmer. She didn't feel like a farmer, and she did not look like any farmer that I had seen. She didn't. And well, sir, this was very big trouble for me, I had some trouble, because even though I thought that I was far enough away to carry on with this girl, I was apparently not far away enough, 'cause I got caught. I got caught by the farmers who lived nearby my house. Them seen me with a girl who was not a farmer pretty much tipped 'em off. Oh, I would say that I had some problems, yes I would."

The room was quiet, then Blake, on his own, without provocation, without pushing, offered a story about himself.

He said, "When I was five, my father taught me how to play the guitar. He was playing in a blues band and a jug band simultaneously, and I would sit on the side, and pluck along, and I got to where I was pretty good. Yeah, I wish I could play better now, but then, with Dad around, I had a lot of confidence. Anyway, one day we went out to the river, a place north of Stubtown, a river that he often went to, and we played music together. The bank of the river was made of round shiny stones that you could skip across the water. And the water was deep right there. Dad stood up with his guitar, and because he had a little wine to drink, he fell over the slippery round stones, that were loose, and he went into the water with his guitar. But the messed-up thing was, he could play the guitar like a top, but he had never taken the time to learn how to swim. And I had never learned either, so I stood on the bank and watched him go under the deep and muddy water. Dad was swept off the little riverbank in slow motion, and quickly began going down into the water, also in slow motion. The guitar was still around his neck and the air escaping from the body of the guitar made bubbles all around him, making it look like he was boiling to death. With an expression fixed on his face that said plainly: I'm getting caught. I suppose the thing that my father was getting caught at was not taking the time to learn how to swim. Finally just the neck of the guitar was sticking up out of the brownish muddy surface, and I remember the last thing visible was his hand still on the neck of the guitar, so panicked that he couldn't move his fingers that were frozen, still playing a D chord. I remember the chord. And to this day, I cannot play in the key of D. All the years I have been playing, all the records, and all the folks I played for, I have never been able to play in the key of D."

Blake's Dad's last D chord

   An Alan Parker light floods through the windows and envelops Blake sitting among the rest of the patients *trying to find out what it was that made them fuck up so badly. What made them. Soon the light is making the entire picture so bright it looks like the whole screen is just going to burn up. Then you notice the dust and scratches on the film, another dimension of the movie screening reality, of: Oh, yeah, it's only a movie with scratched-up clear leader flittering through a projector gate at twenty-four frames per second.*

Godard said that film was truth, twenty-four times a second. Truth-truth-truth-truth-truth . . . that does sound like a projector. That Godard, that old film genius rock star Swiss watchmaker knows his realities.

On Tuesday, Jack calls, and says we should get together and talk.

"About time."

He wants to talk about Time, but first he needs some questions answered. He asks me a few questions about a light meter he says he is holding in his hand. Something about working the light meter. He is still doing things on his own, I realize.

I try to tell him how to use the meter the best that I know how.

He blurts out, "They are building a monument to Felix Arroyo in tha spring outside Las Vegas." He is still blurting. "They are buildin' an amphitheater they want to name after him. You should come over to my house, later. We will be waiting for you."

I get into my car about two hours later. I drive a white Chevrolet with light blue interior that is decomposing quickly. When I sit in the driver's seat I can feel disturbing layers of peeled seat interior rubbing against my leg, scratching me with exposed burlap-like seat stitching. The seat is exposed like a dead animal. There is a twelve-gauge hole blown straight to the floorboards. If I look down I can actually see springs inside the seat as well, and occasionally I drop little things down the hole that I want to get rid of. Little things that are bothering me and are in my way. I never see these things again, not that I want to. I don't want to.

I must have quite a treasure down there by now. I reach into the hole to investigate what treasure there might be. I find one Portuguese escudo, a flat gray coin. Having never been to Portugal, I wonder what it could mean. Was the person who sold me the car Portuguese? This flat coin is almost completely worthless in this country. It is almost completely worthless in the country that it came from. I put it back in the hole.

I find a small square picture of a twelve-year-old girl who is looking directly at me, smiling. She is wearing braces. The picture has a large grease mark that covers half of it and tones the picture randomly. I quickly put it back, not knowing who she is. I can't stop thinking about these sorts of things. It used to bother everyone at work.

When I arrive at Jack's house, the sun has just broken through thick clouds and is blinding me as it shines off the wet sidewalk that leads to Jack and Matt's apartment.

When I am sitting in their apartment, details about time become overlooked because of time's relative unimportance in dimensional travel. There is apparently no time in these other dimensions.

Mistakes that Jack and Matt make are either intentional or else they are learning to travel in these other dimensions before they have received their dimensional-travel air clearance or whatever the fuck.

"The Time mistakes are somewhat common," they reassure. It makes me emotionally unbalanced, and nervous somewhat like jet lag. But I still follow their course.

．　．　．

At one time I ask Jack, "What do you mean you are from another dimension? Why didn't you tell me before?"

He says, "Because. It's a secret."

"What does it mean?" I ask. "Does it mean you are a Spaceman?"

"Yes," Jack says.

"I thought so," I say.

I ask him, "Are you going to bring me there? Why are you talking to all these other filmmakers in town, and showing them your film, why not me?"

Jack pauses and sips from a China Cola.

"Because," he says, "I was testing our technique, then we were going to try it out on you. Sometimes it doesn't work and we lose the person." He holds the palm of his right hand up and places the China Cola in his palm with the other hand. "We care about you."

"Why?"

Jack holds up his hand, as if answering the question is going to get us way off the track. The China Cola drops on the floor, fizzing and gurgling. Jack picks it back up calmly and takes a sip from the wet bottle, finishing with a fizzy snap.

"But anyway," Jack says, "there is no order to how these things fall into place. Timewise, there is no Before, from where we start from. We showed Harris the Cowboy Nemo film before it was finished, although it has always been finished, and also has yet to be started—but showing Harris was our own fuckup."

He smiles. "We're fucked up, dude."

Matt takes a sip of a beer that he has been holding in his hand. I look at them for a bit as they stand, offering themselves for inspection.

Nothing out of the ordinary with their clothing today. Jack has the razor-ripped T-shirt on again, and Matt has the pirate look going again, with a new cap that is an intense Day-Glo orange.

"I'm not supposed to tell you this," Jack says, "but what-the-hey . . ."

He looks at Matt, then back at me. "I have a message from Felix."

"Felix Arroyo?"

"Felix says that he tried to communicate with you but his will isn't strong enough for a special message that is apart from the whole."

"Oh . . ."

"He loves you as much as he can, but he cannot love you very much," Jack finishes.

Jack slaps the palms of his hands together, the China Cola mysteriously missing, and Matt gets up from a stubby-legged chair that he was sitting in on the apartment floor. "So! That's that, and now . . ."

I look at Jack with a confused crinkling of my nose.

"You'll understand later," Jack says.

"Jack?" I say as he walks into an adjoining kitchen off the main living room, needing to raise my voice for him to hear me. "You are testing this dimensional travel on other people before you try it on me?"

Jack is in the kitchen for a moment knocking things around, then comes back into the living room holding an orange, nodding yes.

"And when something goes wrong, the people never come back?"

Jack shakes his head no. "They don't come back."

I am somewhat surprised, and concerned.

"There is a reason that I look like him," Jack says as he peels the orange.

I sit in rapture.

"It's because I am a Felix, but I have been watered down by eternity, which you run into in Pink.

"After having flown through eternity it is hard to be able to put yourself back together enough to have such a particular directive as trying to contact one single person out of billions and billions that you are part of."

I see a book about vaudeville laying partly under a scrappy chair.

"Are you guys into comedy?"

"Vaudeville," Matt says with a kooky smile.

Jack says, "Vaudeville creates a medium of focus. A heightened reality in the electrical atmosphere, or the something! So that you can find a gap into which you can go into the Pink. Do you understand?"

"It's a trick," I say.

"Right on," Matt says.

I sort of understand. I look at Jack with anticipation and a smile.

We get down to business after Jack finishes his orange, letting a little kitten that lives in the apartment lick some of the juice off the ends of his wet fingers.

There is a "dimensional orientation" given by Jack and Matt, for my benefit. We have the orientation around a little square table that has checkers inlaid on the surface. The rest of their living-room furniture has been turned over. Papers are on the floor. I can't remember if the room was as disheveled when we started this session. The checkered table has a sort of cosmic vibe about it.

Then I remember the time when they thought their apartment had been robbed after playing that fast game of basketball; speed basketball or whatever they were playing. They had said the furniture had been overturned and they had no explanation.

They see that I am fixated (sort of scared) with the checkered design on the little square table that has a beer glass sitting on it but they tell me the table doesn't have any relationship to what we are doing, that it is a table they found outside the burned remnants of a tavern next door.

"Then why is it here in the middle of the room, placed so perfectly? Why a table at all?"

"The table is for our comedy routines," Matt says.

They are teaching me about Pink. I am learning slowly. I begin to laugh.

While I am still laughing, Jack informs me that it is both his and Matt's birthday. Do they want presents?

I say, "Happy twenty-third birthday."

Some of their discussions and instructions are mismanaged, I think. But since I don't know what they are doing in the first place I cannot be sure. And they aren't going to tell me either.

They don't want to look like beginners. They are serious about this, I don't think that I have seen them this serious before. Both of their brows are furrowed endearingly. And they occasionally look into my eyes simultaneously with their brows furrowed like that, which is comical, but they are obviously looking for something. Some reaction or transition from me.

There is a great big yellow satchel all of a sudden. It is beautiful. Jack and Matt are communicating with hand signals foreign to me. I remember how Matt used to talk to me with his hands; cutting the air. He uses his hands a lot. The overall image with this yellow bag begins to take on the quality of a Marx Brothers vaudeville sketch.

Specifically the sketch is the one where Harpo will not let the bellboy at a hotel take his bag up to his room. Jack and Matt have the bag in their hands. Jack is trying to take the bag from Matt, but Matt, like Harpo, is acting like the bellboy/Jack is trying to steal his bag.

Matt gets the bag, he puts it down. Jack picks the bag up again, but Matt wrestles the bag back from him.

Pink

233

I am taken with the brightness of the yellow bag. It seems to be getting brighter.

"What's in the bag?" I ask, but realize they cannot hear me, they are so intent on this routine. I begin to laugh loudly.

Occasionally I am concerned that they are really fighting over the bag, but then I realize it is a procedure for my benefit, for my illumination, if you will. I am receiving information.

Jack puts his hands into Matt's pants, his bell-bottomed pirate pants, here we go. He massages Matt's crotch a bit, then gets impatient with the pants, which are in the way, he pulls the pants down, exposing Matt's white and gracefully formed lower body, with his penis halfway erect. Jack works on this, he bends down and begins sucking on Matt's penis.

Matt meanwhile is caressing the back of Jack's head, which is going back and forth in front of Matt's crotch. He is calling him Felix!

"Felix . . ." Matt is groaning. They are loving but they are not in love.

They stop this, and Matt pulls his pants back up.

Did I really see this? A scene from my own life. I am not sure. Alarming as it is. I am having trouble understanding them. Are they blowing this? (Ha-ha.)

They look into my eyes brows a-furrowed. Something happens all at once. I can see now that Jack is a part of Felix. I have heard Matt call Jack "Felix," during this procedure, at least once.

He is him, but Jack is not able to remember the things that Felix would remember. Jack is in turn calling Matt "Blake."

I begin to cry and laugh at the same time. Time, which I can see now, is connected to the immediate, and it is being pulled apart. This is fascinating. To say the least. But it is also occasionally very, uh, flaky. Like a bad magic act.

Who would have guessed that time travel would be like bad dinner theater. Or a bad porno film. Somehow I thought it would have been more . . . apocalyptic. Fabulous. Makes you want to forgive all the bad acting out there.

Jack is working on remembering Felix-things. There seems to be another being in the room. But they are not acknowledging the being. The being is somewhat like a combination of themselves.

Matt falls down. I am reminded of the main plot point of TEEN. Somewhat weird.

The beer glass that was sitting on the checkered table has changed position, it has been moved from one place to another. Matt steps on a rubber squeaky duck and acts afraid of it, funny.

Then there are many beings in the room. Everyone is in the room, again somewhat like a Marx Brothers gag.

One of the reasons that Jack looks like Felix in the

first place is because it is my perception of him, he doesn't look like that to other people, for instance.[53] Really weird. Part of Jack's interest in contacting me in the first place was because of Felix. Felix has come to get me! As promised. But there is more serious business afoot than Felix.

There is an overall pattern, Jack tells me, sweating; although he is somewhat frustrated with the complicated nature of what it is they are up to, and with my passive impatience. But I haven't done anything but sit here.

He tells me to concentrate. Which at this point is something that I want to do . . . They open the bag and little white kittens are walking out, no, they are flowing out, like melted white art nouveau kittens, so weird . . . there is a loud hissing noise before I can complete my thoughts about the kittens.

We are there . . . that is, I am in another dimension. In the Pink.

I am alone, and then again I am not.

It is unlivable. One doesn't live when in the Pink.

If I could describe it, it would be the sensation of being so flat that you can't stand, sit up, or turn. You are like flat. But you do move. And you move wherever you want, or more accurately you are already there, wherever it is you are to be. You are already everywhere, where everything has always been and will always be.

[53] This isn't true. Jack has told Spunky this so that he continues to concentrate when Jack and Matt look into his eyes.

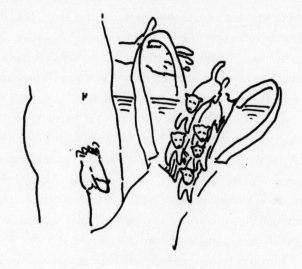

The Kittens

There seems to be no future or past. It is solid (flat) now.

Unexplainable. In four dimensions, however, distance and movement suggest that there is such a thing as the past and future. There is not, only in our electromagnetic universe, which replays the past and future for our benefit and survival. Here in the Pink past and future are connected like a big long solid tree trunk. The Now of our universal dimension could be described as the growth rings that you see when you (unnaturally) cut a slice into the tree trunk. (Now is unnatural, but it is where we exist, no matter.) Here you stay flat. That is as close as I can describe it.

It's unbelievable. I am as flat as a mathematical equation. I feel like an equation. Everybody is here too, yet I am alone. Rather, I am everybody.

Shit! You realize this when you get here. Now, it is going to be funny when I get back (to reality?), having felt the sensation of Pink. If I get back. I can understand Jack and Matt's occasional confusion. Also, Matt's irreverence is suddenly meaningful when in the Pink. He's only playing with time. The girl in San Francisco was right, Time is going backwards.

I used to think that Jack was Felix, and now I see he is. But he is also everyone else. There are no dimensional bodies here. Connections, but not bodies. And the connections remain connected all the time. They do not apply themselves, then disconnect, and reapply. They don't. I am connected. I like it here. I am dead, and I like it. It is good. It is equally good as being alive. At least it is not as unusually cruel as when you are alive.

Am I in bed? But I haven't died. It feels almost like you are alive. It's dark. It is.

Soon after this timeless experience I arrive back into our dimension, skipping backwards. I suppose it is better than going forwards, I don't know what that would be like.

When I leave Jack and Matt's apartment the days click backwards and it becomes last Thursday. And the whole week plays itself all over again. This is because Jack and Matt made a Time mistake, I think, because they weren't paying attention. Or else this is their way to keep me coming back to them again.

For instance, on Thursday I receive a short phone call from the bottled water company, then work a little on $-GREAT SKULL ZERO-$ and after that I go down to the neighborhood bar and watch Harris have a beer, while he is into a deep discussion about his new film project with some of the other local filmmakers you could call Sasquatch Color.

Harris' new film project is to be animated using chalk somehow. I didn't get all of it, because I sat down at the table in the middle of the discussion.

So on Thursday the same events play themselves out all over again. I don't notice but I am repeating these five days of the week, Thursday, Friday, Saturday, Sunday and Monday. I learn that later.

I am unaware that I am repeating the same discussion about the water, then working again on the same passage of $-GREAT SKULL ZERO-$ and after that having a beer and sitting down during the same middle part of Harris' discussion about CHALK.

This puts me in a small four-day loop, which culminates in another visit with Jack and Matt when Tuesday comes around. A human delay loop, playing itself over and over again.

Where are Jack and Matt? They seem busy. I find myself, on this overcast Thursday morning, talking on the phone to the bottled water company that I use. I haven't been paying my bills on time and they want to cancel my service and come to get the water dispenser that sits in my kitchen. I do my best to dissuade them and tell them that I will send a check today. I have only been tardy a few weeks, they are so strict about the payments of five dollars per bottle of water. I need to find some money.

I think that maybe I should quit dreaming, scrap the filmmercial business, and open a store that sells Kitchen Refrigerator Magnets and Other Curios. That suddenly sounds very comforting. Kitchen refrigerator magnets that have toll paintings on them. Also, magnets that have printed fabric bows tied on to them, the kind that are so heavy the magnet barely holds them on the refrigerator. I suppose that everyone is in need of refrigerator magnets, they're useful, so maybe this isn't such a bad idea.

Someone is coming up the front stoop of my house. God! I have visitors.

Jack and Matt are paying a visit, which never happens. I can see them standing on the stoop at the front door of my apartment just before I open the door and they are staring with these furrowed brows. I open the door and they look me up and down almost like a doctor might look at you after you wake up from a coma.

"What's up?"

They shuffle around, not wanting to come in. Jack is holding the light meter that he called me about the other day.

"Hey, what does the green indicator mean, on this dial here, Bro'?"

"That's for low-light situations," I say, and turn a dial on the top of the meter which flips up a small window on the front of the meter, and allows it to suck in more light.

This satisfies them and they decide they should be leaving. They are going to work on their movie.

Right, the movie, I almost forgot.

"What is that movie going to be about anyway?" I ask.

"Muscles . . ." Jack says.

Matt makes a muscle with his arm.

"Muscles . . ." Jack and Matt say together.

"And when do I get to see it?" I ask.

Jack shrugs. "In time, you can see it."

After a moment of leisurely deliberation I go to the Twenty-first Avenue Tavern, the central hangout for all unbusy filmmakers in Sasquatch. The old Twenty-first Avenue Tavern, or Cinema Tavern as it is sometimes known, is just one block away from every local filmmaker's favorite office building. A building where I once had an office, and once had a secretary and some video equipment.

This is an unusual place, in that people sit here all day and talk about film projects and nonprojects and drink beer.

The dreams that these filmmaker friends come up with are so pie-in-the-sky inspiring that I quiver.

Harris is in the middle of the group and has been explaining CHALK, his animated project that he has been working on for three years now. Nobody has ever seen a frame of this film. Like Cowboy Nemo.

Harris turns to me and says, "Spunky? I've been thinking." Harris thinks a lot.

Harris is a creature. I'm a creature too. Our cellular phones touch in the middle of the table.

Joanna sits across the table with her arms folded, listening to Harris.

Harris says, "I have been thinking about sensitive, areas, of, the, body."

I glance around the table at the others. There are three or four others, all with cellular phones touching each other in the middle of the table at the Twenty-first Avenue Tavern.

"Like here," Harris says as he is touching his chest, "here is one sensitive area, a sensitive area of the body." Then he touches his neck. "Yeah, like here, this too, another sensitive area for me. Or here"—he touches his crotch—"another one."

"Definitely," I say.

"Or here." He touches his shins and says, "This is a place that is very sensitive."

Just then one of the phones rings. We glance simultaneously at the cloverleaf pattern of phones in the center of the table. To all of us it could mean we will work today, or it can also be a wrong number. It could be Hollywood calling, which all of us secretly wish would happen, even though we pretend that we could care less. But it is okay, because it never is Hollywood calling. Never. We have played this game before. Which phone is it?

With reserve, we all pick up our respective phones and look at them. You would think that they would give each phone a different ring to it or some way to tell them apart.

It is my phone. It is Jack. Harris is interrupted. Life is a long series of interruptions. Jack wants to meet on Tuesday, he wants to talk about something, wonder what it is. It could be he wants some money, money that I don't have. Maybe Matt wants something. Maybe he wants some new skis, ha-ha.

After I talk with Jack, I ask Harris if he would explain the sensitive areas of the body again like he was doing before the phone rang.

I want him to keep speaking of his vision because when Harris goes on like this, it is one of the most inspiring things I think that I have ever heard. A mind alone, musing about the planets, and sharing its musings with other minds alone. Fascinating. It is quite literally what gives me the energy to keep on riding along with this cockeyed caravan.[54]

All of us sit here day after day waiting for something to happen but nothing ever does. People come, people go, nothing ever happens.[55]

Joanna, aside from animating like a fiend, is planning to make a documentary about the salmon crisis in the Northwest. There are no more salmon running. They could run but they couldn't hide. They can't make it up the fish ladders that circumnavigate the hydroelectric dams that are blocking their way on the river.

Dan[56] is making a low-budget film like the one that Buzz Post made a few years ago. Dan's script is about four

[54] This is a quote Spunky remembers from a Preston Sturges film called *Sullivan's Travels.*

[55] This is a quote Spunky is remembering from the ending of the movie *Grand Hotel.*

[56] Dan is a fixture in the commercial scene in Sasquatch. He had originally started out as a teacher, segueing into dealing used hospital equipment, then got into instructional film production. He has a bright red carrot-topped head that looks like burning flames are leaping from him, and he always wears this one tweed sport coat where he keeps pens in the front breast pocket.

friends, ten years after their college frat days, who decide to get together for a dinner party. They all take LSD at the party, like they did when they are in college, but very soon find out that they can't handle it like they used to; while the film descends into an introspective freakout, the characters search for a way out of the druggy quagmire that they've got themselves into.

"Pretty interesting, Dan," Harris says.

"Yeah, Dan, is that something that happened to you recently?" Joanna asked with a machine-gun laugh jittering out each word from her mouth like she was riding on a washboard.

"No, no, when I take LSD with my old friends, we can *always* handle it," Dan says.

I didn't know Dan was into LSD. How queer.

Dan's concept is not so much like Buzz Post's, which was about friends on a fishing boat, but Dan intends to produce it in much the same manner that Buzz did his film, he explains.

"I see."

"He means, with almost no money," Joanna spitfires comically.

"Exactly," Dan confirms.

Buzz, of course, would obviously no longer sit at this table with us musing about his dreams and his films, because they've already come true. He will stop by to pat us on the back every now and then, offering see-through encouragement of a patronizing nature.

He almost never stops name dropping when he does come by, and it bugs the shit out of all of us, so I guess that it's good that he doesn't hang with us at all, or we might end up trying to strangle him, or something worse.

Some of us are at odds with the idea of trying to make a commercial film to pander to Hollywood or try to be a big star or someone important, and sometimes I am one of them. But you never know. We may get our chance. I may get my chance to sell out and kiss ass. I am sure if that chance ever comes along I will gladly disgrace myself for the meager and worthless notoriety that I now only dream of. Which is why we have this circle of phones in the middle of the table.

We can goof off sitting here in this bar, but at the same time we are reachable by our respective offices and message machines and opportunities.

Jack should be here with us. Matt no doubt will be when he finds out that they serve beer here.

I am listening to the local Christian radio station. I realize its entire play list of music has one thing in common: Jesus. A religious ideology holds the programming together, nothing else. You have rock songs, reggae songs, children's songs, classical songs, all with Jesus in the foreground or the background or all around. I like this programming attitude, and I think that all art should be in the service of something like Jesus, and not in the service of the glory of the artists themselves.

Art used to be more of a community service in the good old days, around Jesus' time. Communal, in the service of one group thought, one group ideology. Now it is a speculative service looking for bucks.

Today we have different art continuity.

Pink

Πινκ αλτ. υνιϖερσ.

There is Eddie. He, like Lonnie, is a friend here on the inside. He is as much of a character as Lonnie, and together we make up a small united group, to help each other, and to stick with the group philosophy, which is not to indulge. Eddie and Lonnie told me they are going to help me bust out of here. I'm getting tired of being here. Eddie is a twenty-one-year-old blond-haired boy with round glasses and big lips. I like him. Eddie, being younger like me, has more difficulty in following through with our group philosophy, he is going to find it hard to find his way from Edge City back to his aboriginal state. He is going to have to work on it. Harder than some of us will. Some of the patients are old, sick and tired of fucking around like they have been, an entire life of fucking around. But this is not the case when you are at your beginning, because at the beginning you have nowhere to go. You don't particularly have any reason to be good. You don't have to stop things. Because you are young and resilient and full of life. Not until things get really bad do you have to do anything about them. And part of the reason that the old people are trying to help themselves is because their bodies are breaking down, and they just can't handle it anymore. We can handle more abuse. So our hearts go out to Eddie, because for him, he can really fall, and mess up his whole junket, his whole life.

He gives me a piece of artwork that he has done. It is a Xerox copy of Jesus Christ. His higher power? One of the things that we have to do in this place is to find a higher power, an entity that we can blame things on and get it off of our own guilt-tripped shoulders. I ask Eddie if his higher power will be Jesus. He tells me that his higher power is going to be vaudeville. Which of course I think is ridiculous. But then I am intrigued. I am interested. Could that work? Is he being a twenty-one-year-old wise guy? Yes. But is that a way to find your higher power? Maybe. He is an artist, and for them, higher powers can be difficult, which is why he ended up here in the first place. This makes me wonder what my higher power is. As I think of it, from what I have been able to find, my higher power is this other dimension I have heard of. The place that always was and always will be. It is the molecular configuration of the floor that I am in contact with.

Cowboy Nemo is finally finished. I have seen it. And it's not half bad. Jack showed it to me on an old squeaky sixteen-millimeter film projector. It was truth. It was truth twenty-four times per second. It was horribly scratched and thumbprinted and torn apart because Jack was projecting the original. It didn't seem like it was a new film at all, more like it had been around forever and had been shown by every student film projectionist in every grade level as a projection training film. That is part and parcel of Jack's art, I suppose.

Whenever I see one of Jack's films it seems very original yet it has a tatteredness about it like he was sending dirt through the gate of the camera before he started shooting.

There was a scene where one of the Cowboy Nemos threw his cowboy hat in the air and lassoed it. The black-and-white film had a restored-old-film quality about it. As if the film had been burned and the restoration consisted of reshooting every frame on a new negative so you can see shrinkage, dust and water marks personalizing every frame, flittering by like broken bird wings in an endlessly complicated display of Pop Art flashes and pops and squiggles and glitches.

Behind the Pop Art glaze, the story unfolds: Nemo is cramped into his apartment above a Thai fast-food restaurant. The smell of food from the Thai and other fast-food joints is in the air of Nemo's hometown. Nemo

1

Cowboy Nemo

lives in what looks like a mall, an endless mall where every block of the city is two or three stories and has little shops with windows glowing neon red and green on the ground floor. People live above the shops.

Nemo is a well-built tanned young cowboy. He has his own secret world that he enters through his dingy corner bedroom closet. Nobody knows about this Nemo world but him. In this other world, there are other well-built tanned young cowboys, but they are from different points in the Universe.

The only language that they have in common is a pidgin language called Envirese. Nemo is issued a small computer, which is embedded in his skull, that helps him with certain facts and figures, like an encyclopedia surgically inserted into his brain. The computer can also capture images and sounds that Nemo hears and can store the information for one hundred days before erasing it. This computer is apparently common to people of the near future like Nemo.

Jack, you can fool me some of the time but not all of the time.

In Nemo Land, everyone goes by the name of Nemo, and so they use Envirese numbers to distinguish themselves, like Ska, which in Envirese is seven, becoming Nemoska, or the number Ola, eight, becoming Nemola. We get to know the other Nemos well (a pitch crutch). To Jack's credit. There is an elaborate sequence of scenes during which the Nemos are orienting themselves to their new life in Nemo Land. Making their bunks, playing cards and making buckaroo coffee. We meet Nemosa, she is a very strong cowgirl with virtually no gender.

There is Nemoti, who is a well-built young and tan Eurasian cowboy. And we have Nemobo, a funny but handsome cowboy. All the Nemos stay in a fantastically large bunkhouse with all the other Nemos.

During cowboy orientation, all the Nemos meet in a football-stadium-sized barn. They do calisthenics in the morning to a song that sounds like it is being performed by Massive Attack.

Jack's story is so funny, it's funnier than I thought it would be. The Nemos have to stand in long lines forever to enter a superpower competition. Together the Nemos compete by lifting huge weights off of the ground with their superpowers, and sometimes they can levitate with some amount of effort.

Nemobo is sent on a mission to go into the distant universe and strange planetary world of Nemoshi's to retrieve him. Nemoshi was the 1989 winner of the Nemo Land competition. When a Nemo wins the competition, he is supposed to stay in Nemo Land and be of service, but this guy Nemoshi escaped through a trapdoor that a janitor in the bunkhouse showed him, and returned home. He is apparently an alcoholic in his hometown karaoke bar. Nemobo drops through the metal Nemo Land refuse eject hole that Nemoshi disappeared through, and he uses colored tags connected with invisible string plus his computer to remember the steps that he takes so he can return the same way.

Nemobo heroically retrieves Nemoshi, against Nemoshi's will, from his hometown bar with much fighting and carrying on with the local Yakuza, but on their return trip from Nemoshi's hometown, Nemobo's computer goes down with an eerie last gasp.

"System . . ." it reports as it dies, "system . . . systemmmmm . . ."

This means that Nemobo has to find his return path through the vast universe using his own memory, carrying Nemoshi, against Nemoshi's will, on his back through an Intergalactic wasteland.

During his journey, Nemobo begins to question existence and identity, and is haunted by a huge chrome Texas Star in the sky that has no explanation. He finds that he can control the giant Chrome Star with his mind, make it change shapes or make it go away altogether.

Confused, he crosses through space with Nemoshi on his back, getting hopelessly lost in a strange dark planetary jungle.

When Nemoshi grows out of his alcoholic indifference, he shows Nemobo which way to get back to Nemo Land.

After they return, a final competition is held to test their strength, and all the Nemos are pitted against a giant 800-foot-tall Nemonster replicant and try to overpower it by flicking themselves at it like fleas.

Nemobo valiantly calls to the Chrome Star in the sky and with his will, and much vortexing and buffeting, he manages to suck the Nemo-800 into the Chrome Tex*Ass Star in a black-blue sky, then make the Chrome Star disappear.

Nemobo wins the Nemo prize, a magic lasso. And has to stay in Nemo Land forever.

The musical soundtrack swells with appropriated classical music and all the Nemos cry for their victories.

Jack's movie is squeaky clean fun. Educational too, the way I like 'em, because you eventually learn how to speak Envirese. I thought I never would, but I did.

Trees die, the forest lives forever

Next day in the Rubber Neck Grill, there are various journeymen filmmakers and hangers-on around a table near the back, near the espresso machine.

Our conversation is punctuated by a loud, very loud, hissing sound every time the waitress needs to make a latte.

Joanna, present and accounted for, is sitting across from me, looking like she has had a bad night, which for Joanna is extremely unusual, she is usually pert and bright, not dark and haggard. She has apparently been up all night editing her Salmon documentary. Harris is also with us, always thinking as usual, and John,[57] a tall introspective character with a full bushy beard and a pipe, who is wearing a beret. John is a producer of informmercials like me.

Besides producing informmercials, John is writing a screenplay on the side; like I am; like we all are; but his screenplay is about a relationship, unlike my supposed action film.

We listen supportively to Joanna as she tells us about the problems she has been having with the Cutlass Power Company. They have lost valuable historic footage of the salmon runs during the twenties and thirties.

[57] John hails from Berkeley, and he has been through the sixties, and the tear gas and the draft card burning, and he still harbors some of that antiestablishment fire within him, but not too much, because he fits right in at Softbox, which is Sasquatch's informmercial production headquarters.

The Historic Society used to have footage, they were sure of it, until Cutlass Power did an unusually large presentation of their future plans to save the salmon. Now the films don't exist. They disappeared.

The head of the Society is thinking of suing Cutlass for losing the valuable material. Cutlass Power Company points out their having created the footage to begin with, partly under the WPA. They even used a Woody Guthrie song on one of the soundtracks, because he wrote a song about the Cutlass Dam.

"It is all so underhanded and corrupt," Joanna says, hitting her hand on the table with a demure plap. "No more salmon, and no more movies of the salmon. As if they never existed!"

I live in a house that was built by a salmon canner and I lower my head visibly, feeling a special hidden guilt. As if I am sheltered from the rain and sun directly by the salmon's misfortune. And I am. Sheltered from the Oregon rain by the fruits of an endangered river creature.

"Unless the salmon can make it back upriver to their original spawning ground," Joanna says, "they do not reproduce. They die without reproducing, but if Cutlass Power tried just a little bit harder, it would make everything . . ."

sssssss . . . the espresso machine overpowers Joanna's last sentence, her mouth moving delicately, finishing a thought, but none of us able to hear.

John smiles and says, "I know what you mean, Joanna."

Πινκ αλτ. υνιϖερσ.

I am lying in a bed in a mansion in a big city. There is a plastic pillow on the bed. And I am thinking and feeling how very fragile life is. All life. Even life that you thought was the strongest thing in the world, suddenly it seems very fragile. With people shooting things, flying around in planes and bungee jumping all over the place. I want to learn about how fragile all the world is. I want to learn about it, so I can try to help it.

Tuesday arrives, and I have been summoned to meet Jack and discuss Time.

It's odd that he calls and promises we will have a discussion.

Sabene, who is wearing a kimono, is with me, in Sasquatch for an informmercial shoot, and he has brought his new friend Vincent[58] along. Again, like before, although I am not aware of it, Matt's apartment is cluttered and the furniture is turned upside down. This time I notice beer bottles lying all over the place. Also, this time, Sabene and Vincent are with me. I only have a feeling of déjà vu, not a memory of having gone through this before.

Jack and Matt are wearing some of the Masonic costuming that must have come from the film school projection room. Matt has a turban on his head and bright yellowish-green shoes that go out in a spiral at the toes, curling back in on the tops of his feet.

There is a Cowboy Nemo poster on the wall. Part of a proposed advertising campaign.

Jack and Matt get right to it. They begin by taking off all of their clothes and kissing each other all over their bodies. Right in front of Sabene, Vincent and me. Neat. Then, while still naked, they do the vaudeville routines all

---

[58] Vincent is a young, blond, sixteen-year-old, heavily built, coltlike boy.

over again, sometimes looking me in the eye with that concentrated furrow of the brow. They do that. They glance now and then at both Sabene and Vincent. Sabene and Vincent too are entangled in some sort of mock routine following Jack and Matt with their clothes off.

More people are in the room, again. The room is now resembling a nudist colony with the nudists playing some crazy volleyball-like game. The faces on the players resemble ones I have seen in an old 1925 staff picture of the William Morris Agency.

Vaudeville was about time. The big time, the small time. Its effectiveness depended on timing.

Jack and Matt doing their comedy routine with the yellow bag

Here is the yellow bag . . . oh, I remember this now. The yellow bag routine, naked yet. Matt's dick swings this way and that as he tugs at the yellow bag that Jack, as the bellboy, is trying to take from him, but the bag opens and is spilling onto the floor . . .

Then, as before, the kittens come a-flowin'. Flowing kittens, silvery white ones, like mercury, and just before they hit the floor, that is it. We are in the Pink.

Dimension, Existence, Culture and Identity all splinter and are left behind.

Pink Sound, brothers and sisters. Pinkness. It's dark. It's . . . flat. It is unexplainable . . . it is peaceful . . . it is love . . .

. . . it is . . .